Praise for *Await Your Reply*

"Chaon's fans will be deeply satisfied by this book, and those who've never read him will get a riveting introduction to one of the great literary minds of our day." —*New York Post*

"Oddly mesmerizing . . . Some novels you read to find out what happens next. Others are appealing more for the trip itself, not how it ends. *Await Your Reply* captures readers both ways."
—*USA Today*

"Ambitious, gripping . . . Chaon is a dark, provocative writer, and *Await Your Reply* is a dark, provocative book; in bringing its three strands together, Chaon has fashioned a braid out of barbed wire."
—*The New York Times Book Review*

"Chaon artfully weaves three tales of people running away into a gripping, satisfying read." —*Entertainment Weekly*

"A literary page-turner, a cunningly plotted and utterly unput-downable novel." —*Publishers Weekly* (starred review)

"With a cliffhanger punctuating the close of nearly every chapter, *Await Your Reply* has the pacing of a thriller. But it is far more elegant, intelligent, and philosophical than the standard fare of that genre. Chaon situates his characters in beautiful, desolate settings . . . and deftly navigates the paradoxes that shape the plot."

—Bookforum.com

"Fascinating . . . Teasing out the truth is one of the numerous pleasures of this fine novel." —*Austin American-Statesman*

"Easily [Chaon's] most ambitious work to date."   —*Kirkus Reviews*

"A page-turning mystery."   —*Pittsburgh Post-Gazette*

"*Await Your Reply* deftly straddles the divide between a well-made thriller, with its elaborate plot and its efficient, telegraphic language, and a more expansive, self-consciously literary meditation on the shifting nature of identity."   —*The Denver Post*

"There is, beneath the [novel's] sheen, a beating heart, and it is a heart worth knowing."   —*Chicago Sun-Times*

"[A] beautifully written, thoughtful novel."

—*San Antonio Express-News*

"Like his first novel, *You Remind Me of Me,* Dan Chaon's latest is a profound and haunting exploration of the shifting, often tenuous, nature of identity. The fact that Chaon has chosen to revisit this theme in the context of a tense, chilling story of modern cybercrime enriches his novel and gives it a disturbingly timely feel. . . . Far more than an absorbing mystery, in this complex and psychologically astute story Dan Chaon puts on a virtuosic display of his literary talent. It is a thrilling example of the best of contemporary literary fiction."   —*BookPage*

"Chaon never fails to impress."   —*Library Journal*

"*Await Your Reply* is a compelling thriller, but it's an existential thriller (written in pitch-perfect prose of calm luminosity) that possesses the intricate concentricities of Borges and the bleak infinities of Lovecraft."   —*The Commercial Appeal*

"*Await Your Reply* manipulates issues of identity crisis and theft in an absorbing narrative that gradually, cleverly plaits together three stories. . . . A deeply disturbing, yet somehow hopeful journey, for Chaon's characters and readers alike."   —*The Washington Times*

"Subtle intersecting stories of a race to find a missing twin, a birth parent and a happy marriage that will make you question your own sense of time and identity."   —*San Francisco Chronicle*

"[*Await Your Reply* is] as involving as a good mystery, moves like a first-rate thriller, and contains a great deal of strange, poetic imagery and insight into the idiosyncrasies of human nature."
     —*PopMatters*

"Excellent . . . a genre-bending thriller, a different and more ambitious effort than his three previous works."   —The Rumpus

"[An] outstanding psychological suspense novel . . . Chaon is so adroit at dropping in his wicked little clues that it might be tempting to begin rereading the book immediately, to try to find the subtleties."   —*Akron Beacon Journal*

"*Await Your Reply* illuminates what it takes to maintain a true identity, on paper and in perception."   —Associated Press

AWAIT YOUR REPLY

AWAIT YOUR REPLY

A Novel

DAN CHAON

BALLANTINE BOOKS TRADE PAPERBACKS

NEW YORK

2010 Ballantine Books Trade Paperback Edition

Published in the United States by Ballantine Books, an imprint of The Random
House Publishing Group, a division of Random House, Inc., New York.

BALLANTINE and colophon are registered trademarks of Random House, Inc.

RANDOM HOUSE READER'S CIRCLE and Design is a registered
trademark of Random House, Inc.

Originally published in hardcover in the United States by Ballantine
Books, an imprint of The Random House Publishing Group,
a division of Random House, Inc., in 2009.

LIBRARY OF CONGRESS CATALOGING-IN-PUBLICATION DATA
Chaon, Dan.
Await your reply : a novel / Dan Chaon.
p. cm.
ISBN 978-0-345-47603-6
1. Identity theft—Fiction.   I. Title.
PS3553.H277A95 2009
813'.54—dc22   2009021245

Printed in the United States of America

www.randomhousereaderscircle.com

2 4 6 8 9 7 5 3 1

Book design by Dana Leigh Blanchette

For Sheila

AWAIT YOUR REPLY

PART ONE

✦━✦

I myself, from the very beginning,
Seemed to myself like someone's dream or delirium
Or a reflection in someone else's mirror,
Without flesh, without meaning, without a name.
Already I knew the list of crimes
That I was destined to commit.

—ANNA AKHMATOVA,
"Northern Elegies"

1

We are on our way to the hospital, Ryan's father says.
Listen to me, Son:
You are not going to bleed to death.

Ryan is still aware enough that his father's words come in through the edges, like sunlight on the borders of a window shade. His eyes are shut tight and his body is shaking and he is trying to hold up his left arm, to keep it elevated. *We are on our way to the hospital,* his father says, and Ryan's teeth are chattering, he clenches and unclenches them, and a series of wavering colored lights—greens, indigos—plays along the surface of his closed eyelids.

On the seat beside him, in between him and his father, Ryan's severed hand is resting on a bed of ice in an eight-quart Styrofoam cooler.

The hand weighs less than a pound. The nails are trimmed and there are calluses on the tips of the fingers from guitar playing. The skin is now bluish in color.

This is about three A.M. on a Thursday morning in May in rural Michigan. Ryan doesn't have any idea how far away the hospital might be but he repeats with his father *we are on the way to the hospital we are on the way to the hospital* and he wants to believe so badly that it's true, that it's not just one of those things that you tell people to keep them calm. But he's not sure. Gazing out all he can see is the night trees leaning over the road, the car pursuing its pool of headlight, and darkness, no towns, no buildings ahead, darkness, road, moon.

2

A few days after Lucy graduated from high school, she and George Orson left town in the middle of the night. They were not fugitives—not exactly—but it was true that no one knew that they were leaving, and it was also true that no one would know where they had gone.

They had agreed that a degree of discretion, a degree of secrecy, was necessary. Just until they got things figured out. George Orson was not only her boyfriend, but also her former high school history teacher, which had complicated things back in Pompey, Ohio.

This wasn't actually as bad as it might sound. Lucy was eighteen, almost nineteen—a legal adult—and her parents were dead, and she had no real friends to speak of. She had been living in their parents' house with her older sister, Patricia, but the two of them had never been close. Also, she had various aunts and uncles and cousins she hardly talked to. As for George Orson, he had no connections at all that she knew of.

And so: why not? They would make a clean break. A new life.

———

Still, she might have preferred to run away together to somewhere different.

They arrived in Nebraska after a few days of driving, and she was sleeping, so she didn't notice when they got off the interstate. When she opened her eyes, they were driving along a length of empty highway, and George Orson's hand was resting demurely on her thigh: a sweet habit he had, resting his palm on her leg. She could see herself in the side mirror, her hair rippling, her sunglasses reflecting the motionless stretches of lichen-green prairie grass. She sat up.

"Where are we?" she said, and George Orson looked over at her. His eyes distant and melancholy. It made her think of being a child, a child in that old small-town family car, her father's thick, callused plumber's hands gripping the wheel and her mother in the passenger seat with a cigarette even though she was a nurse, the window open a crack for the smoke to trail out of, and her sister asleep in the backseat mouth-breathing behind their father, and Lucy also in the backseat, opening her eyes a crack, the shadows of trees running across her face, and thinking: *Where are we?*

She sat up straighter, shaking this memory away.

"Almost there," George Orson murmured, as if he were remembering a sad thing.

And when she opened her eyes again, there was the motel. They had parked in front of it: a tower rising up in silhouette over them.

It had taken Lucy a moment to realize that the place was supposed to be a lighthouse. Or rather—the front of the place, the façade, was in the shape of a lighthouse. It was a large tube-shaped structure made of cement blocks, perhaps sixty feet high, wide at the base and narrowing as it went upward, and painted in red and white barber-pole stripes.

THE LIGHTHOUSE MOTEL, said a large unlit neon sign—fancy nautical lettering, as if made of knotted ropes—and Lucy sat there in the car, in George Orson's Maserati, gaping.

To the right of this lighthouse structure was an L-shaped courtyard of perhaps fifteen motel units; and to the left of it, at the very crest of the hill, was the old house, the house where George Orson's parents once lived. Not exactly a mansion but formidable out here on the open prairie, a big old Victorian two-story home with all the trappings of a haunted house: a turret and wraparound porch, dormers and corbeled chimneys, a gable roof and scalloped shingles. No other houses in sight, barely any other sign of civilization, barely anything but the enormous Nebraska sky bending over them.

For a moment Lucy had the notion that this was a joke, a corny roadside attraction or amusement park. They had pulled up in the summer twilight, and there was the forlorn lighthouse tower of the motel with the old house silhouetted behind it, ridiculously creepy. Lucy thought that there may as well have been a full moon and a hoot owl in a bare tree, and George Orson let out a breath.

"So here we are," George Orson said. He must have known how it would look to her.

"This is it?" Lucy said, and she couldn't keep the incredulousness out of her voice. "Wait," she said. "George? This is where we're going to live?"

"For the time being," George Orson said. He glanced at her ruefully, as if she disappointed him a little. "Only for the time being, honey," he said, and she noticed that there were some tumbleweeds stuck in the dead hedges on one side of the motel courtyard. Tumbleweeds! She had never seen such a thing before, except in movies about ghost towns of the Old West, and it was hard not to be a little freaked out.

"How long has it been closed?" she said. "I hope it's not full of mice or—"

"No, no," George Orson said. "There's a cleaning woman coming out fairly regularly, so I'm sure it's not too bad. It's not abandoned or anything."

She could feel his eyes following her as she got out and walked around the front of the car and up toward the red door of the Lighthouse. Above the door it said: OFFICE. And there was another unlit tube of neon, which said:

NO VACANCY.

It had once been a fairly popular motel. That's what George Orson had told her as they were driving through Indiana or Iowa or one of those states. It wasn't exactly a *resort*, he'd said, but a pretty fancy place—"Back when there was a lake," he'd said, and she hadn't quite understood what he meant.

She'd said: "It sounds romantic." This was before she'd seen it. She'd had an image of one of those seaside sort of places that you read about in novels, where shy British people went and fell in love and had epiphanies.

"No, no," George Orson said. "Not exactly." He had been trying to warn her. "I wouldn't call it romantic. Not at this point," he said. He explained that the lake—it was a reservoir, actually—had started to dry up because of the drought, all the greedy farmers, he said, they just keep watering and watering their government-subsidized crops, and before anyone knew it, the lake was a tenth of what it had once been. "Then all of the tourist stuff began to dry up as well, naturally," George Orson said. "It's hard to do any fishing or water-skiing or swimming on a dry lake bed."

He had explained it well enough, but it wasn't until she looked down from the top of the hill that she understood.

He was serious. There wasn't a lake anymore. There was nothing but a bare valley—a crater that had once held water. A path led down to the "beach," and there was a wooden dock extending out into an expanse of sand and high yellow prairie grass, various scrubby plants that she imagined would eventually turn into tumbleweeds. The remains of an old buoy lay on its side in the wind-blown dirt. She could see what had once been the other side of the lake, the opposite shore rising up about five miles or so away across the empty basin.

Lucy turned back to watch as George Orson opened the trunk of the car and extracted the largest of their suitcases.

"Lucy?" he said, trying to make his voice cheerful and solicitous. "Shall we?"

She watched as he walked past the tower of the Lighthouse office and up the cement stairs that led to the old house.

3

By the time the first rush of recklessness had begun to burn off, Miles was already nearing the arctic circle. He had been driving across Canada for days and days by that point, sleeping for a while in the car and then waking to go on again, heading northward along what highways he could find, a cluster of maps origami-ed on the passenger seat beside him. The names of the places he passed had become more and more fantastical—Destruction Bay, the Great Slave Lake, Ddhaw Ghro, Tombstone Mountain—and when he came at last upon Tsiigehtchic, he sat in his idling car in front of the town's welcome sign, staring at the scramble of letters as if his eyesight might be faulty, some form of sleep-deprivation dyslexia. But no. According to one of the map books he'd bought, "Tsiigeht-chic" was a Gwich'in word that meant "mouth of the river of iron." According to the book, he had now reached the confluence of the Mackenzie and the Arctic Red rivers.

WELCOME TO TSIIGEHTCHIC!

Located on the site of a traditional Gwich'in fishing camp. In 1868 the Oblate Fathers started a mission here. By 1902 a trading post was located here. R.C.M.P. Constable Edgar "Spike" Millen, stationed at Tsiigehtchic was killed by the mad trapper Albert Johnson in the shoot-out of January 30, 1932 in the Rat River area.

The Gwich'in retain close ties to the land today. You can see net fishing year round as well as the traditional method of making dryfish and dry meat. In the winter, trappers are busy in the bush seeking valuable fur animals.

ENJOY YOUR VISIT TO OUR COMMUNITY!

He mouthed the letters, and his chapped lips kept adhering to each other. "*T-s-i-i-g-e-h-t-c-h-i-c,*" he said, under his breath, and just then a cold thought began to unfold in the back of his mind.

What am I doing? he thought. *Why am I doing this?*

The drive had begun to feel more and more like a hallucination by that point. Somewhere on the way, the sun had begun to stop rising and setting; it appeared to move slightly to and fro across the sky, but he couldn't be sure. Along this part of the Dempster Highway, a silvery white powder was scattered on the dirt road. Calcium? The powder seemed to glow—but then again, in this queer sunlight, so did everything: the grass and the sky and even the dirt had a fluorescent quality, as if lit from within.

He was sitting there by the side of the road, his book open in front of him on the steering wheel, a pile of clothes in the backseat, and the boxes of papers and notebooks and journals and letters he had collected over the years. He was wearing sunglasses, shivering a little, his patchy facial hair a worn yellow-brown, the color of a coffee stain. The CD player in his car was broken, and the radio played only a murky blend of static and distant garbled voices. There was no cell phone reception, of course. An air freshener in the shape of a Christmas tree was hanging from the rearview mirror, spinning in the breath of the defroster.

Up ahead, not too far now, was the town of Inuvik, and the wide delta that led to the Arctic Ocean, and also—he hoped—his twin brother, Hayden.

4

The man said, "Above the wrist? Or below the wrist?"

The man had a sleepy, almost affectless voice, the voice you might hear if you called a hotline for computer technical support. He looked at Ryan's father blandly.

"Ryan, I want you to tell your father to be reasonable," the man said, but Ryan didn't really say anything because he was crying silently. He and his father were bound to chairs at the kitchen table, and Ryan's father was shuddering, and his long dark hair fell in a tent around his face. But when he looked up, he had a troublingly stubborn look in his eyes.

The man sighed. He carefully pushed the sleeve of Ryan's shirt up above his elbow and placed his finger on the small rounded bone at the edge of Ryan's wrist. It was called the "ulnar styloid," Ryan remembered. Some biology class he had taken, once. He didn't know why that term came to him so easily.

Above the wrist . . . the man said to Ryan's father . . . *or below the wrist?*

———

Ryan was trying to reach a disconnected state—a *Zen* state, he thought—though the truth was that the more he tried to lift his mind out of his body, the more aware he was of the corporeal. He could feel himself trembling. He could feel the salt water trickling out of his nose and eyes, drying on his face. He could feel the duct tape that held him to the kitchen chair, the strips across his bare forearms, his chest, his calves and ankles.

He closed his eyes and tried to imagine his spirit lifting toward the ceiling. He would drift out of the kitchen, where he and his father were pinned to the hard-backed chairs, past the cluttered construction of dirty dishes piled on the counter by the sink, the toaster with a bagel still peeping up out of it; he would waft through the archway and into the living room, where a couple of black-T-shirted henchmen were carrying computer parts out of the bedrooms, dragging matted tails of electrical cording and cables along behind them. His spirit would follow them out the front door, past the white van they were tossing stuff into, and on down his father's driveway, traveling the rural Michigan highway, the moonlight flickering through the branches of trees as his spirit gained velocity, the luminous road signs emerging out of the darkness as he swept up like an airplane and the patterns of house lights and roads and streams that speckled and crisscrossed the earth growing smaller. *Woooooooooooooooooooo*—like a balloon with the air let out of it, a siren, a wailing wind. Like a person screaming.

He squeezed his eyes, tightened his teeth against one another as his left hand was grasped and tilted. He was trying to think of something else.

Music? A landscape, a sunset? A beautiful girl's face?

"Dad," he could hear himself saying, through chattering teeth. "Dad, please be reasonable, please, please be—"

———

He would not think about the cutting device the man had shown them. It was just a length of wire, a very thin razor wire, with a rubber handle attached to each end of it.

He wouldn't think about the way his father wouldn't meet his eyes.

He wouldn't think about his hand, the wire looped once around his wrist, his hand garroted, the sharp wire tightening. Slicing smoothly through skin and muscle. There would be a hitch, a snag, when it reached the bone, but it would cut through that, too.

5

And Lucy awoke and it was all a bad dream.

She was dreaming that she was still trapped in her old life, still in a classroom in high school, and she couldn't open her eyes even though she knew that there was an asshole boy in the desk behind her who was flicking stuff into her hair—boogers, or possibly tiny rolled-up pellets of chewing gum—but she couldn't wake up even though someone was knocking at the door, a secretary was at the door with a note that said, *Lucy Lattimore, please report to the principal's office. Your parents have been in a terrible accident—*

But no. She opened her eyes, and it was merely an early evening in June, still sunny outside, and she was asleep in front of the television in the alcove room in George Orson's parents' house, and an old black-and-white movie was playing, a videotape she had found in a stack next to the ancient cabinet television set—

"Why don't you stay here awhile and rest, and listen to the sea?" said the lady in the movie.

She could hear George Orson chopping on the cutting board in the kitchen—an intent tapping rhythm that had woven its way into her dream.

"It's so soothing," said the woman in the movie. "Listen to it. Listen to the sea. . . ."

It took Lucy awhile to realize that the tapping had stopped, and she lifted her head and there was George Orson standing in the doorway in his red cook's apron, holding the silver vegetable knife loosely at his side.

"Lucy?" George Orson said.

She sat up, trying to recalibrate, as George Orson tilted his head.

He was handsome, she thought, handsome in a collared-shirt-and-sweater intellectual way that you hardly ever saw back in Pompey, Ohio, with close-cropped brown hair and a neatly trimmed beard and an expression that could be both sympathetic and intense. His teeth were perfect, his body trim and even secretly athletic, though in fact he was, he said, "a little over thirty."

His eyes were a stunning sea-green, a color so unusual that at first she'd assumed it was artificial, some fancy colored contacts.

He blinked as if he could feel her thinking about his eyes.

"Lucy? Are you okay?" he said.

Not really. But she sat up, straightened her back, smiled.

"You look like you've been hypnotized," he said.

"I'm fine," she said. She put her palms against her hair, smoothing it down.

She paused; George Orson gazed at her with that mind reader look he had.

"I'm *fine*," she said.

———

She and George Orson were going to be living in the old house behind the motel, just for a short time, just until they got things figured out. Just until "the heat" was off a bit, he told her. She couldn't tell how much of this was a joke. He often spoke ironically. He could do imitations and accents and quotations from movies and books.

We can pretend we are "fugitives on the lam," he said, wryly, as they sat in a parlor or sitting room, with fancy lamps and wingback chairs that had been draped with sheets, and he put his hand on her thigh, petting her leg with a slow, reassuring stroke. She put her Diet Coke onto a doily on the old coffee table, and a bead of perspiration ran down the side of the can.

She didn't see why they couldn't be fugitives in Monaco or the Bahamas or even the Riviera Maya area of Mexico.

But— "Be patient," George Orson said, and gave her one of his looks, somewhere between teasing and tender, bending his head to look into her eyes when she glanced away. "Trust me," he said in that confiding voice he had.

And so, okay, she had to admit that things could be worse. She could still be in Pompey, Ohio.

She had believed—had been led to believe—that they were going to be rich, and yes of course that was one of the things that she wanted. "A lot of money," George Orson had told her, lowering his voice, lowering his eyes sidelong in that shy conspiratorial way. "Let's just say that I made some . . . *investments*," he said, as if the word were a code that they both understood.

That was the day that they left. They were traveling down Interstate 80 toward this piece of property that George Orson had inherited from his mother. "The Lighthouse," he said. The Lighthouse Motel.

They'd been on the road for an hour or so, and George Orson was in a playful mood. He had once known how to say hello in one hundred different languages, and he was trying to see if he could remember them all.

"*Zdravstvuite,*" George Orson said. "*Ni hao.*"

"*Bonjour,*" said Lucy, who had loathed her two required years of French, her teacher, the gently unforgiving Mme Fournier, repeating those unpronounceable vowels over and over.

"*Päivää,*" George Orson said. "*Konichiwa. Kehro haal aahei.*"

"*Hola,*" Lucy said, in the deadpan voice that George Orson found so funny.

"You know, Lucy," George Orson said cheerfully. "If we're going to be world travelers, you're going to have to learn new languages. You don't want to be one of those American tourist types who assume that everyone speaks English."

"I don't?"

"Not unless you want everyone to hate you." And he smiled his sad, lopsided grin. He let his hand rest lightly on her knee. "You're going to be so *cosmopolitan,*" he said tenderly.

This had always been one of the big things that she liked about him. He had a great vocabulary, and even from the beginning, he'd treated her as if she knew what he was talking about. As if they had a secret, the two of them.

"You're a remarkable person, Lucy." This was one of the first things that he'd ever said to her.

They were sitting in his classroom after school, she had ostensibly come to talk about the test for the next week, but that had faded away fairly quickly. "I honestly don't think you have anything to worry about," he'd told her, and then he waited. That smile, those green eyes.

"You're different from other people around here," he said.

Which was, she thought, true. But how did *he* know? No one else in her school thought so. Even though she did better than anyone else in the entire school on the SAT, even though she earned A's in nearly all her classes, no one, neither teachers nor students, acted as if she were "remarkable." Most of the teachers resented her, they didn't really like ambitious students, she thought, students who wanted to leave Pompey behind, and the other students thought that she was a freak—possibly crazy. She hadn't been aware that she had the habit of muttering sarcastic things under her breath until she discovered that quite a number of people in her school thought that she had Tourette's syndrome. She didn't have any idea where or when such a rumor had started, though she suspected that it might have originated with her honors English teacher, Mrs. Love-joy, whose interpretations of literature were so insipid that Lucy could barely contain—or apparently had failed to contain—her scorn.

But George Orson, on the other hand, actually liked to hear what she had to say. He encouraged her ironic view of the great figures of American history, actually chuckled appreciatively at some of her comments while the other students stared at her with stern boredom. "It's clear that you have a brilliant mind," he wrote on one of her papers, and then when she came to see him after class to talk about the upcoming exam he told her that he knew what it was like to be different—misunderstood—

"You know what I'm talking about, Lucy," he said. "I know you feel it."

Perhaps she did. She sat there, and let him turn his intense green eyes on her, an intimate, oddly probing look, both ironic and heartfelt at the same time, and she drew in a small breath. She was well aware that she was not regarded as pretty—not in the conventional world of Pompey High School, at least. Her hair was thick and wavy, and she could not afford to have it cut in a way that made it more manageable, and her mouth was too small and her face was too long. Though maybe in a different context, she'd imagined hopefully, in a different time period, she might have been beautiful. A girl in a Modigliani painting.

Still, she wasn't used to being looked in the eye. She fingered the silk scarf she was wearing, an item she'd found in a thrift store, which she thought might have a slight Modigliani quality, and George Orson regarded her thoughtfully.

"Have you ever heard the term 'sui generis'?" he said.

Her lips parted—as if this were a test, a vocabulary word, a spelling bee. On the wall were various inspirational social studies posters. ELEANOR ROOSEVELT, 1884–1962: "NO ONE CAN MAKE YOU FEEL INFERIOR WITHOUT YOUR CONSENT." She shook her head, slightly uncomfortable.

"I don't know," she said. "Not really."

"That's what you are, I think," George Orson said. "Sui generis. It means 'one of a kind.' But not in the phony, feel-good, self-help way—everyone is an individual, blah, blah, blah, just to boost the self-esteem of the mediocre.

"No, no," he said. "It means that we invent ourselves. It means that you're beyond categories—beyond standardized test scores, beyond the petty sociology of where you're from and what your dad does and what college you get into. You're outside of that. That's what I recognized about you right away. *You invent yourself*," he said. "Do you know what I mean?"

They looked at each other for a long time. Eleanor Roosevelt waved down at them, smiling, and a hope tightened inside her, like a warm, soft fist. "Yes," she said.

Yes. She liked that idea: *You invent yourself.*

They were making a clean break. A new life. Wasn't that what she'd always wanted? Maybe they could even change their names, George Orson said.

"I get a little tired of being George Orson," he told her conversationally. They were driving through the middle of Illinois in his Maserati with the top down and her unmanageable hair was rippling behind her and she was wearing sunglasses. She was gazing critically at herself in the side mirror. "How about you?" George Orson said.

"How about me, what?" Lucy said. She lifted her head.

"What would you be if you weren't Lucy?" George Orson said.

Which was a good question.

She hadn't answered him, though she found herself thinking about it, imagining—for example—that she would like to be the type of girl who had the name of a famous city. *Vienna,* she thought, that would be pretty. Or *London,* which would be wry and vaguely mysterious, in a tomboyish way. *Alexandria:* proud and regal.

"Lucy," on the other hand, was the name of a mousy girl. A comical name. People thought of the television actress, with her slapstick ineptitude, or the bossy girl in the *Peanuts* comic strip. They thought of the horrible old country song that her father used to sing: "You picked a fine time to leave me, Lucille."

She would be glad to be rid of her name, if she could think of a good replacement.

Anastasia, she thought. *Eleanor?*

But she didn't say anything because a part of her thought that such names might sound a little vulgar and schoolgirl-ish. Names that a low-class girl from Pompey, Ohio, would think were elegant.

One of the nice things about George Orson was that he didn't know much about her past.

They didn't talk, for example, about Lucy's mother and father, the car wreck the summer before her senior year, an old man running a stoplight while the two of them were on their way to the Home Depot to buy some tomato plants that were on sale. Killed, both of them, though her mother had lingered for a day in a coma.

The fact that people at school had known about it had always felt like an invasion of privacy. A secretary had given Lucy condolences, and Lucy had nodded, graciously she thought, though actually she found it kind of repulsive that this stranger should know her business. *How dare you,* Lucy thought later.

But George Orson had never said a word of condolence, though she guessed that probably he knew. He knew the basics, anyway.

He knew, for example, that she lived with her sister, Patricia, though Lucy was relieved that he had never actually seen her sister. Patricia, herself only twenty-two, not very bright, Patricia who worked at the Circle K Convenient Mart most nights and with whom, since the funeral, Lucy had less and less contact.

Patricia was one of those girls that people had been making fun of for almost all the years of her life. She had a thick, spittley lisp, easily imitated and cartoonish, a bungler's speech impediment. She wasn't fat exactly, but lumpy in the wrong places, already middle-aged-looking in junior high, with an unfortunately broad, hen-like figure.

Once, in grade school, they were walking to school together and some boys chased them, throwing pebbles.

> *Patricia, Patrasha,*
> *Has a great big ass-a!*

the boys sang.

And that had been the last time that Lucy had walked with Patricia. After that, they had begun to go their separate ways once they left for school, and Patricia had never said anything; she had just accepted the fact that even her sister wouldn't want to walk with her.

After their parents died, Patricia had become Lucy's guardian— perhaps officially still was? Though now Lucy was almost nineteen. Not that it mattered in any case, because Patricia had no idea where she was.

She did feel a pang about that.

She had the image of Patricia and her pet rats—the rats' cages stacked in the eaves, and her sister coming home late from her job at the Circle K, kneeling there in that red and blue vest with the name tag that said PATARCIA, talking to the rats in that crooning voice, the one rat, Mr. Niffler, with an enormous tumor coming out of its stomach that it was dragging around and her sister had paid to have the veterinarian remove it and then it *grew back,* the tumor, and still Patricia persisted. Showering the dying creature with love, buying it plastic toys, talking baby talk, making another appointment at the vet.

Lucy was glad that she had never told George Orson about Mr. Niffler, just as she was glad that he'd never seen the house she had grown up in, where she and Patricia had continued to live. Her father used to call it "the shack," affectionately. "I'll meet you back here at the shack," he'd say when he left for work in the morning.

It didn't occur to her until later that it *was* basically a shack. Ramshackle, haphazard, a living room and kitchen that bled into each other, the bathroom so cramped that your legs touched the edge of the bathtub when you sat on the toilet. A garage stuffed with car parts, bags of beer cans that her father never took to the re- cycling center, the hole in the plasterboard wall of the living room through which you could see the bare two-by-fours, the carpet that looked like the fur of a worn-out stuffed animal. Some stairs led up to an attic, where the girls, Lucy and Patricia, had their beds. The ceiling of the bedroom was the roof, which slanted sharply over them while they slept. If George Orson had seen it, she imagined, he would have been embarrassed for her; she would have felt dirty.

Though—she couldn't say that she was particularly happy to be *here,* either.

In the middle of the night, she found herself wide awake. They were in the old bed of George Orson's parents, a king-size expanse, and she was aware of the other rooms in the house—the other empty bedrooms on the second floor, the trickle of a pipe in the bathroom, the toothy rows of bookshelves in the "library," the flutter of birds in the dead trees of the high-fenced backyard. A "Japanese garden," George Orson called it. She could picture the small wooden bridge, the bed of stunted, un-flowering irises choked with weeds. A miniature weeping cherry tree, still barely alive. A granite Kotoji lantern statue. George Orson's mother had had an "artistic bent," he'd told Lucy.

By which he meant, Lucy assumed, that his mother had been a little crazy. Or so Lucy gathered. The place—the motel and the house—seemed as if it had been put together by someone with multiple personality disorder. A lighthouse. A Japanese garden. The living room with its gruesome old sheet-covered upholstery, and the room with the television and the big picture window that looked out onto the backyard. The kitchen with its 1970s colors, the avocado-green stove and refrigerator, the mustard-colored tile floor, drawers and cabinets full of dishes and utensils, an old wooden butcher block and an almost obscenely large collection of knives—George Orson's mother had apparently been obsessed with them, since they could be found in almost every shape and length a person could imagine, from tiny filet blades to enormous cleavers. Very disturbing, thought Lucy. In a pantry, she found three boxes of china dishes and some disturbing canning jars, still full of dark goop.

On the second floor, there was the bathroom and three bedrooms, including this one she was in right now, the very room, the very bed where his parents had slept, where his elderly mother had continued to sleep, Lucy imagined, after the husband had died. Even now, many years later, there was still a vague hint of old-lady powder about it. A few hangers still in the closet, and the empty dresser sitting darkly against the wall, and then the stairs that led up to the third floor—to the turret, a small octagon-shaped room with a single window, which looked out away from the lake, out onto the cone of the faux lighthouse, and the courtyard of motel rooms. And the highway. And the alfalfa fields. And the far distant horizon.

And so—she couldn't help it, she couldn't sleep, and she lay there staring up at the swimmy darkness that her brain couldn't quite process. The door was closed, the window shade was pulled, so there wasn't even moonlight or stars.

Suggestions of shapes floated across the surface of the dark like protozoa seen through a microscope, but there wasn't too much for the optic mechanisms to actually hold on to.

She slid her hand beneath the covers until she came up against the shoreline of George Orson's body. His shoulder, his chest, the ribs rising and falling underneath his skin, his warm belly, which she pressed against—until at last he turned over and put his arm over her, and she felt her way along the length of it until she found his wrist, his hand, his pinkie finger. Which she held.

Okay.

Everything would be fine, she thought.

At the very least, she wasn't in Pompey any longer.

6

Miles's twin brother, Hayden, had been missing for more than ten years, though probably "missing" wasn't exactly the right word.

"At large"? Was that a better term?

When the most recent letter from Hayden arrived, Miles had pretty much decided that it was time to give up. He was thirty-one years old—they were both thirty-one years old—and it was time, Miles thought, to let go. To move on. So much energy and effort, he thought, squandered, pointless. For a while Miles felt a new determination: he was going to live his own life.

He was back again in Cleveland, where he and Hayden had grown up. He had an apartment on Euclid Heights Boulevard, not far from their old house, and a job managing a store called Matalov Novelties, an old storefront mail-order establishment on Prospect Avenue that dealt primarily in magicians' equipment—flash paper and smoke powder, scarves and ropes, trick cards and coins and top hats and so forth, though they also sold joke gifts and gags, useless gadgets, risqué toys, some sex stuff. The catalog was somewhat unfocused, but he liked that. He could organize it, he thought.

Was it what he had hoped to do with his life? Probably not exactly, but he had a good brain for receipts and orders, and he felt a certain affection for the stock on the shelves, the carnival aura of the trashy occult and bright plastic legerdemain. There were times, sitting at the computer in the dim windowless back room, when he thought it wouldn't be a bad career after all. He had grown fond of the old proprietress, Mrs. Matalov, who had been a magician's assistant back in the 1930s, and who now, even at ninety-three, had the stoic dignity of a beautiful woman who was about to be cut in half. He had a good rapport with Mrs. Matalov's granddaughter, Aviva, a sarcastic young woman with dyed black hair and black fingernails and a narrow, sorrowful face, whom Miles had begun to imagine he could probably ask out on a date.

He had been thinking about going back to college, maybe getting a degree in business. Also, possibly, getting some short-term cognitive therapy.

So when Hayden's letter arrived, Miles was surprised at how quickly he had fallen back into his old ways. He shouldn't have even opened the letter, he thought later. And in fact, when he came home to his apartment building that day in June and opened the mail cubbyhole and saw it there among the bills and flyers—he actually decided that he should leave it unopened. *Set it aside,* he thought. *Let it rest for a while before you look at it.*

But no, no. By the time he had gone up the three flights of stairs to his apartment, he had already torn open the seal and unfolded the letter.

My Dear Miles, it said.

Miles! My brother, my best beloved, my only true friend, I'm sorry that I have been out of touch for so long. I hope you don't hate me. I can only pray that you understand the grave situation I have found myself in since we last spoke. I have been in deep hiding, very deep, but every day I thought about how much I missed you. It was only my fear for your own safety that kept me from contact. I am fairly certain that your phone lines and email have been contaminated, and in fact even this letter is a great risk. You should be aware that someone may be watching you, and I hate to say this but I think you may actually be in danger. Oh, Miles, I wanted to leave you alone. I know that you are tired of all of this and you want to live your own life, and you deserve that. I'm so sorry. I wanted to give you the gift of being free of me, but unfortunately they know we are connected. I have just lost someone very dear to me, due to my own carelessness, and now my thoughts turn to you with great concern. Please be wary, Miles! Beware of the police, and any government official, FBI, CIA, even local government. Do not have any contact with H&R Block or with anyone representing J.P. Morgan, Morgan Stanley, Goldman Sachs, Lehman Brothers, Merrill Lynch, Chase, or Citigroup. Avoid anyone associated with Yale University. Also, I know that you have been in contact with the Matalov family in Cleveland, and all I can tell you is DO NOT TRUST THEM! Do not tell anyone about this letter! I hate to put you in an awkward position, but I urge you to get out of Cleveland as soon as possible, as quietly as possible. Miles, I am so sorry to have involved you in all this, I truly am. I wish I could go back and do things differently, that I could have been a better brother to you. But that chance is gone now, I know, and I fear that I won't be in this world much longer. Do you remember the Great Tower of Kallupilluk? That may be my final resting place, Miles. You may never hear from me again.

I am, as always, yours, your one true brother,
and I love you so much.

Hayden

So.

What does a person do with a letter such as this? Miles sat there for a while at the kitchen table, with the letter spread out in front of him, and opened a packet of artificial sweetener into a cup of tea. *What would a normal person do?* he wondered. He imagined the normal person reading the letter and shaking this head sadly. *What could be done?* the normal person would ask himself.

He looked at the postmark on the envelope: *Inuvik, NT, CANADA X0E 0T0.*

"I'm going to have to take some personal time, unfortunately," Miles told Mrs. Matalov the next morning, and he sat there with the phone pressed to his ear, listening to her silence.

"Personal time?" said Mrs. Matalov, in her old-fashioned vampire accent. "I don't understand. What does this mean, personal time?"

"I don't know," he said. "Two weeks?" He looked at the itinerary he had planned out on the computer, the map of Canada with a green highlighter mark running a jagged, rivering way across the country. Four thousand miles, which would take, he calculated, approximately eighty-four hours. If he drove fifteen or sixteen hours a day, he could be in Inuvik by the weekend. It might be difficult, he thought, but then again didn't truck drivers do it all the time? Weren't they always making marathon drives such as this? "Well," he said. "Maybe three weeks."

"Three weeks!" Mrs. Matalov said.

"I'm really super sorry about this," Miles said. "It's just that— something urgent has come up." He cleared his throat. "A private matter," he said. *Do not trust the Matalov family,* Hayden had said, which was crazy, but Miles felt himself pause.

"It's complicated," he said.

Which it was. Even if he were to be completely honest, what would he say? How could he ever explain the ease with which these old longings had come back to him, the lingering ache of love and duty?

Perhaps to a therapist it would seem simply compulsive—after all this time, after all the years that he had already wasted—but here, nevertheless, came that same urgency he'd felt when Hayden had first run away from home all those years ago. That same certainty that he could find him, catch him, help him, or at least get him locked up somewhere safe. How could he explain how badly he wanted this? Who would understand that when Hayden left, it was as if a part of himself had vanished in the middle of the night—his right hand, his eyes, his heart—like the Gingerbread Man in the fairy tale, running away down the road: *Come back! Come back!* If he were to tell this to someone, he would seem as crazy as Hayden himself.

He had thought that he was past such feelings, but, well. Here he was. Packing his things. Taking the milk out of his refrigerator and pouring it down the drain. Sifting through his old notes, printing out long-ago emails that Hayden had sent him—the various hints and clues of his whereabouts dropped into fantastical descriptions of invented landscapes, the angry rants about human overpopulation and the international banking conspiracy, the late-night suicidal regrets. And then Miles sat at his desk examining with a magnifying glass the envelope of the letter that Hayden had just sent him, that postmark, that postmark. Rechecking the directions. He knew where Hayden was going.

And now he was almost there.

Miles sat in his car by the side of the road, casually reading through one of Hayden's journals as he waited for the ferry that would take him across the Mackenzie River. Some rails ran up from the slate-gray muddy bank and into the green wrinkled lobes of tundra, but otherwise there wasn't much sign of human habitation. A toilet house. A diamond-shaped road sign. The river was a calm reflective surface, silver and sapphire blue. Once he was across, it was only about eighty miles to Inuvik.

Inuvik was one of the places Hayden had gotten fixated on.

"Spirit cities," he called them, and he had written extensively about Inuvik, among other places, in the journals and notebooks that Miles now had in his possession. For years now, Hayden had been taken with the idea that Inuvik was the site of a great archaeological ruin, that on the edge of Inuvik was the remnants of the Great Tower of Kallupilluk, which had been a spire of ice and stone, approximately forty stories tall, built around 290 B.C. at the behest of the mighty Inuit emperor, Kallupilluk—a figure whom Hayden believed he had contacted once in a past life.

None of this was true, of course. Very few of the things Hayden was obsessed with had much basis in reality, and in the last few years he had strayed even further into a mostly imaginary world. In actuality, there had never been a tower or a great Inuit emperor named Kallupilluk. In real life, Inuvik was a small town in the Northwest Territories of Canada with a population of around thirty-five hundred people. It was located on the Mackenzie Delta—"nested," according to the town's website, "between the treeless tundra and the northern boreal forest," and it had existed for less than a century. It had been constructed building by building by the Canadian government as an administrative center in the western Arctic, incorporated at last as a village in 1967. It wasn't even, as Hayden seemed to believe, on the shores of the Arctic Ocean.

Nevertheless, Miles couldn't help but think of Hayden's drawings of that great tower, the simple but vivid pencil sketch Hayden had done, reminiscent of the Porcelain Tower of Nanjing, and he felt a small, dizzy quiver of anticipation pass through him as the Mackenzie River ferry appeared on the horizon, approaching. Miles had spent a good portion of his life poring over Hayden's various journals and notebooks, and even longer living with Hayden's various delusions. Despite everything, there remained a tiny core of credulity that glowed a little brighter as he came closer to the town of Hayden's fantasies. He could almost picture the place at the edge of the town where the Great Tower once rose up out of the folds of tundra, stark against the wide, endlessly shining sky.

———

This had always been one of the problems: this was maybe one way to explain it. For years and years and years, Miles had been a willing participant in his twin brother's fantasies. Folie à deux, was that what they called it?

Since their childhood, Hayden had been a great believer in the mysteries of the unknown—psychic phenomenon, past lives, UFOs, ley lines and spirit paths, astrology and numerology, etc., etc. And Miles was his biggest follower and supporter. His listener. He had never personally believed in such stuff—not in the way that Hayden appeared to—but there had been a time when he had been happy to play along, and perhaps for a while this alternate world had been a shared part of their brains. A dream they'd both been having together.

Years later when he came into possession of Hayden's papers and journals, Miles was aware that he was probably the only person in the world capable of translating and understanding what Hayden had written. He was the only one who could make sense of those stacks of composition notebooks—that tiny block-letter handwriting; the text and calculations that ran from edge to edge and top to bottom of each page; the manila envelopes full of drawings and doctored photographs; the maps Hayden had torn out of encyclopedias and covered with his geodetic projections; the lines across North America that converged at places like Winnemucca, Nevada, and Kulm, North Dakota, and Inuvik in the Northwest Territories; the theories, increasingly serpentine and involuted, a hodgepodge of crypto-archaeology and numerology, holomorphy and brane cosmology, past-life regression and conspiracy theory paranoia.

My work, as Hayden had at some point begun to call it.

Miles often tried to remember when Hayden first began to use that term: "My work." At first it had just been a game the two of them were playing—and Miles even remembered the day they had started. It was the summer that they turned twelve, and the two of them had been poring over books by Tolkien and Lovecraft. Miles had been particularly fond of the maps that were included in the novels of *The Lord of the Rings,* while Hayden had been more inclined toward the mythologies and mysterious places in Lovecraft—the alien city beneath the Antarctic Mountains, the prehistoric cyclopean cities, the accursed New England towns.

They had found one of those old gold-leaf hard-bound atlases, 25 x 20, on the shelf in the living room with the *World Book Encyclopedia,* and they had loved the feel of it, the sheer weight, which made it feel like it could be some ancient tome. It had been Miles's idea that they could take some of the maps of North America and turn them into fantasy worlds. Dwarf cities in the mountains. Scorched goblin ruins on the plains. They could invent landmarks and histories and battles and pretend that in the olden days, before the Indians, America had been a realm of great cities and magical elder races. Miles thought it would be fun to make up their own Dungeons and Dragons game with real places and fantasy places intermingled; he had some very specific ideas about how this would develop, but Hayden was already bending over the map with a black ink pen. "Here is where some pyramids are," Hayden said, pointing to North Dakota, and Miles watched as he drew three triangles, right there on the page of the atlas. In ink!

"Hayden!" Miles said. "We can't erase that. We're going to get in trouble."

"No, no," Hayden said coolly. "Don't be a fag. We'll just hide it."

And this was one of those early secrets that they had—the old atlas hidden beneath a stack of board games on a shelf in their bedroom closet.

Miles still had the old atlas, and as he waited there at the edge of the river for the ferry to come, he took it out and paged through it once again. There, on the northern coast of Canada, was the tower that Hayden had drawn, and Miles's own clumsy attempt at calligraphy: THE IMPATRABLE TOWER OF THE DARK KING!

How ridiculous, he thought. How depressing—that he should still be following the lead of his twelve-year-old self—an adult man! Over the years that he had been looking for Hayden, he had often thought about trying to explain his situation. To the authorities, for example, or to psychiatrists. To people he had become friends with, to girls he had liked. But he always found himself hesitating at the last minute. The details seemed so silly, so unreal and artificial. How could anyone actually believe in such stuff?

"My brother is very troubled." That was all he ever managed to tell people. "He's very—ill. Mentally ill." He didn't know what else could be said.

When Hayden first started to exhibit symptoms of schizophrenia, back when they were in middle school, Miles didn't really believe it. It was a put-on, he thought. A prank. It was like the time when that quack guidance counselor decided Hayden was a "genius." Hayden had thought this was hilarious.

"Geeenious," he said, drawing the word out in a dreamy, mocking way. This was at the beginning of seventh grade, and it was late at night, they were in their bunk beds in their room, and Hayden's voice wafted down through the darkness from the top bunk. "Hey, Miles," he said in that flat, amused voice he had. "Miles, how come I'm a genius and you're not?"

"I don't know," Miles said. He was nonplussed, perhaps a bit hurt by the whole thing, but he just turned his face against his pillow. "It doesn't matter that much to me," he said.

"But we're identical," Hayden said. "We have the *exact* same DNA. So how can it even be possible?"

"It's not genetic, I guess," Miles had said, glumly, and Hayden had laughed.

"Maybe I'm just better at fooling people than you are," he said. "The whole idea of IQ is a joke. Did you ever think about that?"

When his mother started bringing in the psychiatrists, Miles thought about that conversation again. *It's a joke,* he thought. Knowing Hayden, Miles couldn't help but think that the therapist their mother consulted seemed awfully gullible. He couldn't help but think that Hayden's so-called symptoms came across as melodramatic and showy, and, Miles thought, easy to fake. Their mother had remarried by that time, and Hayden hated their new stepfather, their revised family. Miles couldn't help but think that Hayden was not above using an elaborate ploy—even to the point of imitating a serious illness—just to stir up trouble, just to hurt their mother, just to amuse himself.

Was he faking it? Miles had never been sure, even as Hayden's behavior became more erratic and abnormal and secretive. There were times, lots of times, when his "illness" felt more like a performance, an amplified version of the games they had been playing all along. The "symptoms" Hayden was supposedly exhibiting, according to the therapist—"elaborate fantasy worlds," "feverish obsessions," "disordered thoughts," and "hallucinatory perceptual changes"—these were not so much different from the way Hayden usually behaved when they were deeply involved in one of their projects. He was, perhaps, a little more exaggerated and theatrical than usual, Miles thought, a little more *extreme* than Miles felt comfortable with, but then again there were reasons. Their father's death, for example. Their mother's remarriage. Their hated stepfather, Mr. Spady.

When Hayden was institutionalized for the first time, he and Miles were still working on their atlas pretty regularly. It was a particularly complicated section—the great pyramids of North Dakota, and the destruction of the Yanktonai civilization—and Hayden couldn't stop talking about it. Miles remembered sitting there at dinner one night, his mother and Mr. Spady watching stonily as Hayden pushed the food around on his plate as if arranging armies on a model battlefield. "Alfred Sully," he was saying, talking in a low, rapid voice as if reciting memorized information before a test. "General Alfred Sully of the United States Army, 1st Minnesota Infantry, 1863. Whitestone Hills, Tah-kah-ha-kuty, and there are the pyramids. Snow is falling on the pyramids and he's amassing his armies at the foot of the hill. 1863," he said, and pointed at his boneless chicken breast with his fork. "Khufu," he said, "the second pyramid. That's where he first attacked. Alfred Spady, 1863—"

"Hayden," their mother said, sharply. "That's enough." She straightened in her chair, lifting her hand slightly as if she'd considered slapping him, the way you might a hysterical person who is raving. "Hayden! Stop it! You're not making any sense."

That wasn't true, exactly. He *was* making some sense—to Miles at least. Hayden was talking about the Battle of Whitestone Hill, near Kulm, North Dakota, where Colonel Alfred Sully had destroyed a settlement of Yanktonai Indians in 1863. There were no pyramids, obviously, yet what Hayden was describing was fairly clear, and even quite interesting to Miles.

But their mother was unnerved. The things Hayden's therapist had been reporting had upset her, and later, after Hayden had gone back upstairs and when she and Miles were washing dishes, she spoke in a low voice. "Miles," she said, "I need to ask you a favor."

She touched him lightly, and a piece of soapsuds transferred to his forearm, the bubbles slowly disintegrating.

"You need to stop enabling him, Miles," she said. "I don't think he would get nearly so stirred up if you didn't encourage it—"

"I'm not!" Miles said, but he withdrew from her reproachful look. He wiped his fingers over his arm, the wet spot where she had touched him. Was Hayden sick? he wondered. Was he pretending? Miles thought uncomfortably about some of the things Hayden had been saying recently.

"I'm thinking that I might have to eventually kill them," Hayden had said, his voice in the darkness of the bedroom late at night. "Maybe I'll just destroy their lives, but they actually might have to die."

"What are you talking about?" Miles had said—though obviously he knew who Hayden was referring to, and he felt a little frightened; he could feel the pulse of a vein in his wrist and could hear the soft tiptoeing sound of it in his ears. "Man," he said, "why do you have to say crap like that? You're making people think you're crazy. It's so *extreme*!"

"Hmmm," Hayden said. His voice curled sideways through the dark. Floating. Musing. "You know what, Miles?" he said at last. "I know about a lot of stuff that you don't know about. I have powers. You realize that, don't you?"

"Shut up," Miles said, and Hayden laughed, low, that wistful, teasing chuckle that Miles found both comforting and galling at the same time.

"You know, Miles," he said. "I really am a genius. I didn't want to hurt your feelings before, but let's face it. I'm a lot smarter than you, so you need to listen to me, okay?"

Okay, Miles thought. He believed and he didn't believe, both at the same time. That was the condition of his life. Hayden was a schizophrenic, and he was faking. He was a genius, and he had delusions of grandeur. He was paranoid, and people were out to get him. All of these things were at least partially true at the same time.

In the years since Hayden had gone missing—slipping out of the psychiatric hospital where he had been confined—he had become more and more elusive, harder and harder to recognize as the brother that Miles had once loved so dearly. Eventually, perhaps, that old Hayden would disappear entirely.

If he was, in fact, a schizophrenic, he was one with an unusually practical streak. He covered his tracks skillfully, moving stealthily from place to place, changing his name and identity, managing, along the way, to hold down various jobs and appear, to the people he met, convincingly normal. Personable, even.

Miles, on the other hand, had been the one to live a life of near-vagrancy. He had been the one who must have come across as "feverish" and "disordered" and "obsessive" as he trailed behind Hayden's various aliases. Too late, he came to Los Angeles, where Hayden had been working as a "residual income stream consultant" named Hayden Nash; too late in Houston, Texas, where he had been employed as a computer services technician for JPMorgan Chase & Co., named Mike Hayden. Too late, Miles arrived in Rolla, Missouri, where Hayden had been masquerading at the university as a graduate student in mathematics named, cruelly, Miles Spady.

Too late, also, at Kulm, North Dakota, not far from the White-stone Hill Battlefield historical site, not far from the place where Hayden had once imagined *the great pyramids of the Dakota . . . the Giza, Khufu, and Khafre . . .* It was February, and fat flakes of snow fell on the windshield, the wipers flapping like big wings as Miles imagined the shape of the pyramids emerging out of the gray blur of snowfall. They weren't really there, of course, and neither was Hayden, but at the Broken Bell Inn in nearby Napoleon, a motel clerk—a sullen pregnant young woman—frowned over the enlarged grainy photo of Hayden.

"Hmmm," she said.

From the photo, it would have been difficult to guess that they were identical twins. The picture had been taken years ago, not long after they had turned eighteen, and Miles had gained quite a bit of weight since then. Who knew, maybe Hayden had as well. But even in childhood they had never been truly indistinguishable. There was an aspect of Hayden's face—brighter, more avid, friendlier—something that people responded to, and an aspect of Miles's that they didn't. He could see it in the motel clerk's expression.

"I think I recognize him," the girl said. Her eyes flicked from the photo to Miles and then back. "It's hard to say."

"Take another look," Miles said. "It's not a very good photo. It's fairly old, so he may have changed over the years. Does it bring to mind anyone you've seen?"

He looked down at the photo with her, trying to see it as she might. It was a Christmas photo. It was that horrible winter break, their senior year in high school, that had ended with Hayden institutionalized once again, but in the picture Hayden looked completely sane—a kind-eyed, smiling teenage boy in front of a tinselly tree, his hair a bit shaggy, but no sign whatsoever in his face of the trouble that he was causing—would continue to cause. The girl's mouth moved slightly as she looked at it, and Miles wondered if perhaps Hayden had kissed her.

"Take your time," Miles said, firmly, remembering episodes of a police procedural he'd seen on television.

"Are you a policeman?" the girl said. "I'm not sure if we're supposed to give out that information."

"I'm a relative," Miles said reassuringly. "He's my brother, and he's been missing. I'm just trying to locate him."

She examined the photo a little longer, then at last came to a decision.

"His name is Miles," she said, and she gave him a brief but hooded look, which made him wonder if she was simply being recalcitrant, choosing not to reveal some important tidbit of information she had decided to hold back for no other reason but that she didn't like him as much as she liked Hayden. "Cheshire was his last name, I think. Miles Cheshire. He seemed like a great guy."

He remembered how his heart had contracted when she'd said this, when she'd repeated his own name back to him. It *was* just a joke, he thought then—a complicated, nasty prank that Hayden was engaged in. *What am I doing?* he thought. *Why am I doing this?*

That had been almost two years ago, that trip to North Dakota. He had packed up his things and driven back home, darkly aware that the whole Kulm adventure had been nothing but an elaborate tease. Hayden had been in one of his mean and jolly manic moods, and when Miles got back to his apartment, there was a book waiting for him: *No Tears for the General: The Life of Alfred Sully,* and an 8 x 12 manila envelope that contained an article torn from the pages of *The Professional Journal of American Schizophrenia,* a passage highlighted in yellow marker. "If one twin develops schizophrenia, the second twin has a 48% chance of developing it as well, and frequently within one year of the first twin." There was also an email waiting for him from generalasully@hotmail.com, just one more cheerful dig. "Oh, Miles," it said. "Do you ever wonder what people think of you going around with your posters and crummy old photos and your sad story about your crazy evil twin brother? Do you ever think that people are going to take one look at your raggedy-looking self and they aren't going to tell you anything? They'll think: *Why, it's actually Miles who is the crazy one.* They'll think: *Maybe he doesn't even have a twin brother! Maybe he's just out of his mind!*"

That was it, Miles had thought then, reading the email and blushing with humiliation. He was so furious that he'd thrown the book about Alfred Sully out the window of his apartment, where it landed with an unsatisfying flutter in the parking lot. That was it! he promised himself. They were finished. No more of my time—no more of my heart!

He would forget about Hayden. He would get on with his own life.

He remembered this resolution. It came back to him vividly, even as he sat there in the car, unshaven, unshowered, sorting through the flyers that he'd printed up on simple, durable card stock. HAVE YOU SEEN ME? at the top. Then the photograph of Hayden. Then: REWARD! Though that was probably stretching the truth a little.

He angled the rearview mirror and examined himself critically. His eyes. His expression. Did he look like a crazy person? *Was* he a crazy person?

This was the eleventh of June. 68° 18' N, 133° 29' W. The sun wouldn't set again for about five weeks.

7

In the waiting area of Enterprise Auto Rental, Ryan checked through his identification materials again. Social security card. Driver's license. Credit cards.

All the flotsam that proved that you were officially a person.

In this particular case, Ryan was officially Matthew P. Blurton, age twenty-four, of Bethesda, Maryland. Ryan didn't think that he looked like he was twenty-four, but no one had ever questioned him, so he supposed that he must not look suspicious.

He sat there politely, thinking about a song that he was learning on the guitar. He could picture the tablature in his mind, and his fingers moved inconspicuously as he thought of the positions on the frets, the ham of his hand on his thighs, palm up, the fingers posed into various combinations like sign language.

He knew that he ought to be paying more attention; he was going to screw things up if he didn't take better care. That's what Jay—his father—would probably tell him.

———

And so he lifted his head to see what was going on.

At the counter, there was a middle-aged African American woman in a navy-blue coat and a small purple hat, and Ryan observed her surreptitiously as she withdrew a billfold from her purse.

"My grandmother is ninety-eight years old!" the lady was saying. She regarded her billfold as if she were playing a game of pinochle, frowning, then withdrew a bent ancient-looking credit card. "Ninety-eight years old!"

"Mmmm-hmmm," said the young man behind the counter, who was also African American. The young man's eyes were on the computer screen, and he typed out a burst of letters onto the keyboard.

"Ninety-eight years old," he said. "That's a long time to be alive!"

"It certainly is," the woman said, and Ryan could sense that they were on the verge of settling into a comfortable conversation. He glanced down at his watch.

"I wonder how long my lifeline is," the young man at the computer mused, and Ryan watched as the woman nodded.

"Only the Lord knows," the woman said.

She set her credit card and driver's license upon the counter.

"You know," the woman said, "it's not easy at that age. She doesn't talk much at all anymore, but she does sing a lot. And prays. She prays, you know."

"Mmmm-hmmm," the young man said, and typed again. "Does she have amnesia?" he said.

"Oh, no," the woman said. "She remembers things okay. She recognizes the folks that she wants to, at least!"

They both laughed at this, and Ryan found himself smiling with them. And then—at least partly because he was stupidly smiling at an eavesdropped conversation—he felt lonely.

Back home in Iowa, where he'd grown up, there were practically no black people to speak of, and he'd noticed since coming east that it seemed like black people were always nice to one another, that there was a camaraderie. Maybe that was a stereotype, but still he felt an unexpected sense of longing as the man and woman chuckled. He had an idea about ease, warmth, that private sense of connection. Is that what it was really like? He wondered.

Lately, he had been thinking about contacting his parents, and there was a letter he had in his mind. *"Dear Mom & Dad,"* obviously.

"Dear Mom & Dad, I'm sorry that I haven't been in touch in so long, and I thought I should let you know that I'm okay. I'm in Michigan—"

And then, right, they would want to know, or they would figure out. *"I'm in Michigan with Uncle Jay, and I know that he is my biological father, so I guess that is one thing we can stop pretending about—"*

Which started already to sound hostile. *"I'm in Michigan with Uncle Jay. Staying here for a while until I get some things figured out for myself. I'm writing some songs, earning some money. Uncle Jay has a business venture that I've been helping him out with—"*

Bad idea to even mention "business venture." It came off immediately as shady. *Jay?* they would think. What was the nature of this "business"? Immediately they would think drugs or something illegal, and he had already promised Jay that he wasn't going to tell anyone.

"Swear to God, Ryan," Jay had said as they sat on the couch in the cabin in Michigan, playing video games together. "I'm serious. You've got to swear that you're not going to breathe a word of any of this."

"You can trust me," Ryan said. "Who am I going to tell?"

"Anybody," Jay said. "Because this is extremely, extremely serious stuff. Serious people could become involved, if you know what I mean."

"Jay," Ryan said, "I understand. Really."

"I hope you do, buddy," Jay said, and Ryan nodded earnestly, though truthfully he didn't understand much about the project they were engaged in.

He knew that it was illegal, obviously, a scam of some sort, but the actual purpose was elusive. One day he'd be Matthew P. Blurton and he'd rent a car in Cleveland and then drive the car to Milwaukee and return it at the airport, and then he'd board a plane in Milwaukee using an ID card for Kasimir Czernewski, age twenty-two, and fly to Detroit, and then later, online, he'd transfer bank funds in the amount of four hundred dollars from Czernewski's bank account in Milwaukee to the account of Frederick Murrah, fifty, of West Deer Township, Pennsylvania. Was it simply a very complex shell game, one person sliding into the next person and so on down the line? He assumed that there must be financial gain involved somehow, but if so he hadn't seen evidence of it yet. He and Jay lived in basically a hut in the woods, a little hunting lodge, lots of top-notch computer equipment but very little else of value as far as he could tell.

But Jay looked so serious and stern. He had straight shoulder-length hair, surfer hair, Ryan thought, black with a few threads of early gray running through it, and the droopy army surplus clothes of a teenage runaway. It was hard to imagine him projecting an attitude that wasn't mellow, but suddenly he was startlingly fierce.

"Swear to God, Ryan," Jay said. "I'm serious," he said, and Ryan nodded.

"Jay, trust me," Ryan said. "You trust me, don't you?"

And Jay said, "Sure I do. You're my son, right?" And then he gave Ryan that grin that, despite himself, Ryan still found pretty dazzling, even breathtaking, like he'd almost got a crush or something— *You're my son,* and that deliberate eye contact, both unnerving and flattering, and Ryan, all flustered, was like:

"Yeah, I guess I am. I'm your son."

This was one of the things that they were still figuring out—how to talk about this stuff—and it was all still very uncomfortable, they would start to talk about it, and then neither one of them knew what to say, it required a certain language that was either too analytic or too corny or embarrassing.

The basic fact was this: Jay Kozelek was Ryan's biological father, but Ryan had only found out recently. Up until a few months ago, Ryan had thought that Jay was his uncle. His mother's long-estranged younger brother.

Ryan's existence had been due to the usual teenage mistakes; that was the short version. Two sixteen-year-olds getting carried away in the back of a car after a movie. This was back in Iowa, and the girl's, the mother's—Ryan's mother's—family was strict and religious and didn't believe in abortion, and Jay's older sister, Stacey, wanted a baby but she had something wrong with her ovaries.

Jay had always felt that honesty was called for, but Stacey hadn't felt that it was a good idea at all. She was ten years older than Jay, and she didn't think very highly of him in any case—in terms of his morals, his ideas about life, the drugs, etc.

There's a time and place, she had told Jay, back when Ryan was a baby.

And then later she said: *Why does it matter to you, Jay? Why does it always have to be about you? Can't you think of someone else besides yourself?*

He's happy, Stacey said. *I'm his mom and Owen is his dad and he's happy with that.*

Not long afterward, they had stopped talking to each other. Jay had had some run-ins with the law, and they had argued, and that was that. Jay was hardly mentioned when Ryan was growing up—and then only as a negative example. *Your uncle Jay, the jailbird.* The hobo. Never owned anything he couldn't carry. Got involved in narcotics when he was a teenager and it ruined his life. Let that be a warning. Nobody knows where he is anymore.

And so Ryan hadn't learned the truth—that Stacey was actually his biological aunt, that his little-seen uncle Jay was his "birth father," that his biological mother had committed suicide in her sophomore year in college many years ago, when Ryan was a three-year-old kid living in Council Bluffs, Iowa, with his supposed parents, Stacey and Owen Schuyler, and Jay was backpacking around South America—

Ryan hadn't learned all of this until he was himself in college. One night Jay had called him up and told him all about it.

He was himself a sophomore in college, just like his real mother had been, and maybe that was why it struck such a blow. *My whole life is a lie,* he thought, which he knew was melodramatic, adolescent, but he woke up that morning after Jay had called him and he found himself in his dorm, a corner room on the fourth floor of Willard Hall, and his roommate, Walcott, was asleep under a mounded comforter in the narrow single bed beneath the window, and a gray light was coming in.

It must have been about six-thirty, seven in the morning. The sun wasn't up yet, and he rolled over and faced the wall, chilly old plaster with many thin cracks in the beige painted surface, and he closed his eyes.

He hadn't slept much after his conversation with Uncle Jay. *His father.*

At first it was like a joke, and then he thought, *Why is he doing this, why is he telling me this?* though all he said was, "Oh. Uh-huh. Wow." Monosyllabic, his voice ridiculously polite and noncommittal. "Oh, really?" he said.

"I guess it's just something I thought you ought to know," Jay told him. "I mean it's probably better if you don't say anything to your parents, but you can make your own decision about that. I just thought—it seemed wrong to me. You're a man, you're an adult, I feel like you have a right to know."

"I appreciate that," Ryan said.

But once he'd spent a few hours sleeping on and off, once he'd turned over the facts in his mind a few hundred times, he wasn't sure what he was supposed to do with the information. He sat up in bed and fingered the edges of his blankets. He could imagine his parents—his "parents," Stacey and Owen Schuyler, asleep, back in the house in Council Bluffs, and he could picture his own room down the hall from theirs, the books still on their shelves and his summer clothes still in the closet and his turtle, Veronica, sitting on her rock underneath her heat lamp, all of it like a museum of his childhood. Maybe his parents didn't even think of themselves as fakes, maybe most of the time they didn't even remember that the world they had created was utterly false at its core.

The more he thought about it, the more everything began to feel like a sham. It wasn't just his own faux family, it was the "family structure" in general. It was the social fabric itself, which was like a stage play that everyone was engaged in. Yes, he saw now what his history teacher meant when she talked about "constructs," "tissues of signs;" "lacunae." Sitting there in his bed, he was aware of the other rooms, rows and stacks of them, the other students, all of them housed here waiting to be sorted and processed into jobs and sent down their various paths. He was aware of the other teenage boys who had slept in this very room, decades and decades of them, the dormitory like a boxcar being filled and refilled, year after year, and briefly he could have risen up out of his body, out of time, and watched the generic stream of them entering and exiting and being replaced.

He got out of bed and took his towel off the bedpost and figured he might as well go down the hall to the communal bathroom and shower, and he knew he had to get a grip on himself and study for his chemistry test, he was earning a D, C- at best, *Oh God,* he thought—

And maybe it was at that moment that he broke loose from his life. His "life": it felt suddenly so abstract and tenuous.

He had originally just gone out for coffee. It was by that time around seven-thirty in the morning, but the campus was still sleepy. From the sidewalk he could hear the music students in their carrels, the scales and warm-up exercises mingling dissonantly, clarinet, cello, trumpet, bassoon, winding around one another, and it felt like a fitting sound track, like the music you hear in a movie when the character is about to have a mental breakdown and they clutch their forehead in anguish.

He did not clutch his forehead in anguish, but he did think, once again—

My whole life is a lie!

There were many things to be troubled by in this situation, many things to feel angry and betrayed about, but the one that for some reason Ryan felt most keenly was the death of his biological mother. *My God!* he thought. *Suicide. She* killed *herself!* He felt the tragedy of it wash over him, though now it was past. Still, it outraged him that Stacey and Owen hadn't cared whether or not he knew about this. That they found out about it and tsked, and he was probably in the living room in front of the television, three years old, watching some trite and educational program, and they might have shaken their heads and thought what a favor they had done for him, raising him as their own, all the money and effort they'd put into turning him into the kind of kid who could get a scholarship to Northwestern University, into the type of person who could take his place in the top tier, how hard they had worked to mold him. But there was no indication they ever *contemplated* revealing the truth about his parentage, no indication that they realized that this was *important*, no sense that they understood how badly they had wronged him.

Maybe it was melodramatic, but nevertheless he could feel it sink down through the center of his stomach, that fluttery feeling of epinephrine releasing itself. Part of this was also the upcoming chemistry test, which it was likely he was going to fail, and part of it was that it was one of those cold, tinny mornings in October, very windy, and a school of leaves went scampering into Clark Street like lemmings and were run over by a fast-moving car. It made him think of a term he had read in his psychology class. "Fugue state." Maybe it was the combination of the discordant arpeggios from the conservatory and the leaves in the street. "Fugue." A dissociative psychological state marked by sudden, unexpected travel away from home or one's customary place of work, with inability to recall one's past, confusion about personal identity, or the assumption of a new identity, or significant distress or impairment.

Which actually sounded very interesting, very appealing in some ways, although he supposed that if you *decided* to have a fugue state, it wasn't a true fugue state.

He was also failing psychology.

And there were some issues of minor misappropriation of funds, his student loan, and there had been a letter from the registrar: PAST DUE. DEMAND FOR PAYMENT. It would be very difficult to explain to his parents what he had done with that money, how he had managed to forget about paying his tuition, and instead had frittered the borrowed cash away on things like clothes and CDs and dinner at the Mexican place on Foster Ave. How had it happened? He couldn't even say.

And so now here he was in his rented Chevy Aveo driving through the darkened corridor of Interstate 80 in late January and thinking that he would write a song about driving down the interstate alone and no one knows my name and I am so far away from you, or something like that. But not so corny.

Dear Mom and Dad, I realize that the choices I have made recently haven't been exactly sensitive toward you, and I'm sorry for the pain I have caused. I know that I should have contacted you sooner. I realize that at this point the police are involved and that I am probably considered a "missing person," and I want you to know that it wasn't my intention to bring trouble and sorrow into your life. But here I have done it.

Right now I am standing in a motel lobby in _____, and on the wall of the manager's cubicle is this xeroxed sign, one of those kinds of Wise Sayings that people are always taping up on the wall above their computer or whatever, for some reason.

The sign says:

The circumstances of life—
The events of life—
The people around me in life—
*Do not **make** me the way I am.*
*They **reveal** the way I am.*

*And I find myself here thinking about how much you, Mom, would like that saying, how it might be the thing you would tell me if you could hear all my excuses. I can imagine that I have **revealed** who I am to you all of the sudden and that it has turned out to be an unpleasant surprise. I am not the son you wanted when you took me in as a baby and raised me as your own and tried to turn me into a good person. But I guess I am something else. I don't know what yet but—*

But here he was checking into the motel because he was supposed to have one lodging charge on the Matthew P. Blurton MasterCard and here was a Holiday Inn with free wireless Internet, and he had to check Matthew P. Blurton's email and log in to Instant Messenger and see if Jay might be trying to get in touch.

He had a Matthew P. Blurton cell phone as well, but Jay was cautious about cells and so he was never supposed to call Jay, never supposed to call the house.

He kept worrying that his mother would track him down. She had claimed for years that she didn't even know Jay's whereabouts, but if her son was missing, honestly missing, wouldn't she finally break down and try to locate Jay? Wouldn't she feel that Jay—his true father—had a right to know? For most of the months, he had been staying at the cabin in the woods of Michigan with Jay, sleeping on the couch and going on "quests," as Jay called them, whatever they were doing with the credit cards and the social security numbers and the various lists from the Internet, and it felt like the right thing to be doing even though he sometimes imagined Stacey and Owen back in Council Bluffs.

Sitting at the kitchen table, pressing the tines of their forks into one of Stacey's casseroles, lifting a bite. They had always been one of those silent-dinner-table families, even though Stacey insisted all through high school that they *had to* eat together, as if that somehow made them closer, to sit there side by side shoveling food into their mouths until at last Ryan could tilt away from his cleaned plate and say, "Dad, may I be excused?"

Was she sad now? Ryan wondered. Was she worried and terrified and weepy? Or was she enraged?

There had been that one time in high school when he had fucked up, he had been involved with what Stacey thought of as an "inappropriate" girlfriend and he had been skipping school and generally telling lies and sneaking around, and she had acted with such icy swiftness, sending him off to a wilderness program for recalcitrant juveniles, packing him off in the middle of the night with only a duffle bag, the men, the "counselors," standing at the front door waiting to hustle him into the van and carry him off to a two-week-long disciplinary self-help brainwashing session.

He thought about that, too. He could imagine his mother's resolve, her anger, sending out minions to bring him to ground and drag him back to the life that he'd fled.

Ryan sat there at the desk in his room in the Holiday Inn and opened up his laptop. It was probably not useful to dwell on such things, but he nevertheless found himself typing his own name into the search engine and looking again at some of the old articles and such. For example:

No Developments in Case of Missing College Student

CHICAGO—Chicago police have come to a standstill in the case of a Northwestern University college student who disappeared without a trace in the morning hours of October 20. Following one anonymous lead, divers searched the frigid

Lake Michigan waters near the campus but came up empty-handed. Police Sgt. Rizzo said the investigation has come to a standstill, and there have been no new developments.

—which did make him feel guilty, but it was also disappointing. The cops were clearly not particularly good at their jobs. "Without a trace!" Christ! It wasn't as if he were in disguise. It wasn't as if someone had put a burlap bag over his head and spirited him away in a van or whatever. He walked off campus and took the el downtown to the bus station, and there were certainly plenty of people who saw him that day. Were people so inattentive? Was he that nondescript?

And the suicide angle also bothered him—how quick they were to send divers into the lake! That was his mother's doing, he thought. She knew that his biological mother was a suicide, and didn't it figure that was the first thing she thought of.

It had probably been on her mind for a while, he thought. Every time he talked to her on the phone, she was always asking how he felt, why was he so quiet, was there anything wrong, and he saw now the connections that she had been making all along.

There was a ping as someone signed on to Instant Messenger, and he glanced down because it was about time for Jay to contact him—they always had a brief conversation on IM when he was on these trips, just to touch base, but when he opened up the IM window, it was gibberish.

Or actually, someone was typing in what he guessed was Cyrillic. Russian?

490490: Раскрытие способностей к телекинезу с помощью гипноза . . . данном разделе Вашему вниманию предлагается фрагменты видеозаписей демонстраций парапсихологических явлений.

He regarded this string of characters. Was there a problem with Jay's computer? Was it some obscure joke that Jay was playing? Then he typed:

BLURTON: How about trying it in English, dude?

The cursor sat blinking. Breathing. Then:

490490: Господин Ж??? J???

How freaky, he thought.

BLURTON: Jay??

No answer. 490490 had grown silent, though it felt like a kind of watchful silence, a stillness in the motel room, the curtains pulled closed and the television's slate face staring coolly at the bed, and the distant sound of semis passing on the interstate beyond the motel. He thought maybe he should close the IM window.

But then 490490 began to type again.

490490: Mr J. So good to find Mr J. I see were u r.

8

Lucy woke and she was alone in bed. There was the crumpled space where George Orson had been sleeping, the indented pillow, the blankets pulled aside and she sat up as the room loomed over her. The sunlight rimmed the edges of the curtains, and she could see the watchful closet door and the dark stern shape of the bureau dresser and the half-light reflections in the oval vanity mirror, movement, which she realized was herself, alone in the bed.

"George?" she said.

Nearly a week had passed and still they were here at the old house in Nebraska and she was starting to feel a little anxious, though George Orson had tried to be reassuring—"Nothing to be concerned about," he said. "Just a few things that have to be sorted out. . . ."

But he didn't explain further than that. Ever since they'd arrived, he'd made himself scarce. Hours and hours locked in the downstairs room he called "the study." She had actually kneeled in front of the locked door and fit her eye to the keyhole beneath the cut-glass doorknob, and she could see him as if through a pinhole camera, sitting behind the big wooden desk hunched over his laptop, his face hidden behind the screen.

And naturally it had occurred to her that something had gone wrong with their plan.

Whatever the "plan" was.

Which, Lucy realized, she was not that clear about.

She pulled aside the drapes, and the light came in and that felt a bit better. There was a dry, earthy basement smell that was particularly noticeable in the morning, waking up, a taste of underground in her mouth, a taste of rotten fabric, and the windows didn't open, they were painted shut, and it was clear that the house had been sitting in its own dust for a long time. "I've had an exterminator in, don't worry," George Orson had told her, "and a cleaning woman— once every few months. The place has never been *abandoned,*" he said, a bit defensively, but all Lucy wanted to know was how long it had been since someone had actually lived in the house, how long since his mother had died?

And he estimated, reluctantly.

"I don't know," he said. "Probably about—eight years?" She didn't know why he acted as if even a simple question were an invasion of his privacy.

But a lot of their conversations had been like that lately, and she lingered at the window in her oversize T-shirt and panties looking down at the gravel road that led from the garage past the house and the tower of the lighthouse and the courtyard of the motel units to the two-lane blacktop that ribboned its way eventually back to the interstate.

"George?" she said, more loudly.

She padded down the hallway, and then she went downstairs to the kitchen and he wasn't there, either, though she saw that his cereal bowl and spoon had been washed and placed neatly into the dish drain.

And so she went out of the kitchen and through the dining room to "the study—"

"Study." Which, to Lucy, sounded British or something, pretentious, like some old murder mystery.

The Study. The Billiard Room. The Conservatory. The Ballroom.

But he wasn't there, either.

The door was open and the room was curtained and carpeted and there was a chandelier made of brass with dangling glass dewdrops.

"That was my mother's idea of elegance," George Orson had told her when he showed her the room for the first time and she'd folded her arms over her chest, taking it in. His mother's "idea" of elegance, she assumed, was not *real* elegance—though to Lucy it was in fact fairly impressive. Beautiful oriental carpet, gold-leaf wallpaper, heavy wooden furniture, shelves full of books—not junky paperbacks, either, but real hardcover books with thread-bound spines and thick pages and a dense, woody smell.

Was there a difference, she wondered, some fine distinction of good taste or breeding that would make it okay to call a room a "study" but not okay to have a light fixture that is called a "chandelier"?

There were a lot of things she had yet to learn about social class, said George Orson, whose college days at Yale had sensitized him to such things.

So what did it say about her that her own experience of chandeliers, studies, and so on was so limited? She herself had come from a long, long line of poor drudgers, Irish and Polish and Italian peasants—nobodies, stretching back for generations.

You could draw her family in two dimensions, like characters in a comic strip. Here was her father, a plumber, a kindly, beer-bellied, muddy little man with hairy hands and a bald head. Her mother: windblown and stern, drinking coffee at the kitchen table before she went off to work at the hospital, a nurse but only a licensed practical nurse, just a vocational degree. Her sister, simple and round like her father, dutifully washing dishes or folding a basket of clothes and not complaining as Lucy sat moodily, lazily, on the couch reading novels by the latest young female authors and trying to emanate an air of sophisticated irritation—

She couldn't help but think of her lost, sadly cartoonish family as she looked around the empty study. Her old loser life, which she had left behind for this new one.

In the study was an old oak desk, six drawers on either side, all of them locked. And a file cabinet, also locked. And George Orson's laptop, password protected. And a wall safe, which was hidden behind a framed picture of George Orson's grandparents.

"Grandpa and Grandma Orson," George Orson had said, referring to the grim pair, their pale faces and dark clothes, the woman with one light-colored eye and one dark—"called heterochromia," said George Orson. "Very rare. One blue eye. One brown eye. Probably hereditary, though my grandmother always said it was because her brother hit her in the eye as a child."

"Hmmm," Lucy had said, and now, alone in the room, she regarded the picture once again, the way the woman fixed her heterochromatic gaze on the photographer. A frankly unhappy and almost pleading look.

And then she unhooked the latch the way that George Orson had shown her, and the old photo swung out like a cabinet door to reveal the nook in the wall with the safe.

"So," Lucy had said when she first saw it. The safe had appeared to be quite old, she thought, with a combination wheel like a dial on an antique radio. "Aren't you going to open it?" she said, and George Orson had chuckled—though a bit uncertainly.

"I can't, actually," he said.

Their eyes met, and she wasn't exactly sure what to make of his expression.

"I haven't been able to figure out the combination," he said. Then he shrugged. "I'm sure it's empty, in any case."

"You're sure it's empty," she said. And she looked at him and he held her gaze, and it was one of those moments in which his eyes said, *Don't you trust me?* And her eyes said, *I'm thinking about it.*

"Well," George Orson said. "I doubt very seriously whether it's full of gold doubloons and gems."

He gave her that dimpled half smile of his.

"I'm sure the combination will turn up somewhere in the files," he said, and touched her leg playfully with the tip of his index finger, as if for good luck.

"Somewhere," he said, "if we can find the key to the filing cabinet."

But now, standing in the study, she couldn't help but take another look at the safe. She couldn't help but reach out and test the brass and ivory handle just to be sure that, yes, it was still locked and sealed and impenetrable.

Not that she would steal from George Orson. Not that she was obsessed with money—

But she had to admit that it was a concern. She had to admit that she was very much looking forward to leaving Pompey, Ohio, and being rich with George Orson, and probably it was true that this was part of the attraction of this whole adventure.

In September of her senior year of high school, two months after her parents' deaths, Lucy was just a depressed student in George Orson's Advanced Placement American history class.

He had been a new teacher, a new person in their town, and it was obvious even on the first day of class that he had a *presence*, with his black clothes and his uncanny way of making eye contact with people, those green eyes, the way he smiled at them as if they were all doing something illicit together.

"American history—the history that you have learned up until now—is full of *lies*," George Orson told them, and he paused over the word "lies" as if he liked the taste of it. She thought he must be from New York City or Chicago or wherever, he wouldn't stay long, she thought, but actually she did pay more attention than she was expecting to.

And then in study hall she heard some boys talking about George Orson's car. The car was a Maserati Spyder, she had noticed it herself, a tiny silver convertible big enough for only two people, almost like a toy.

"Did you get a look at it?" she overheard a boy saying—Todd Zilka, whom Lucy loathed. He was a football player, a big athletic person who was nevertheless the son of a lawyer and did well enough in school that he had been inducted into the National Honor Society, after which Lucy herself had stopped going to meetings. If she had been braver, she would have resigned, denounced her membership. In middle school, it had been Todd Zilka who had started calling her "Lice-y"—which wouldn't have been such a big deal except that she and her sister actually *had* contracted head lice, pediculosis, and were dismissed from school in shame until the infestation could be cleared up, and even years later people still called her "Lice-y," it might be the only thing they remembered about her when their twenty-year reunion rolled around.

"Toddzilla," was Lucy's own private name for Todd Zilka, though she did not have the power to make such a name stick on him.

The fact that a creature like Toddzilla could thrive and become popular was one good reason to leave Pompey, Ohio, forever.

Nevertheless, she listened surreptitiously as he spouted his stupid opinions to his idiotic friends in study hall. "I mean," he was saying, "I'd like to know where a crummy high school teacher gets money for a car like that. It's like, an Italian import, you know? Probably costs seventy grand!"

And, despite herself, that gave her pause. Seventy thousand dollars was an impressive amount of money. She thought again of George Orson standing in front of them in the classroom, George Orson in his tight black shirt talking about how Woodrow Wilson was a white supremacist and quoting Anaïs Nin:

"We see things not as they are, but as we are. Because it is the 'I' behind the 'eye' that does the seeing."

And then one afternoon not long later, Toddzilla raised his hand and George Orson gestured toward him, hopefully. As if they might be about to discuss the Constitution together.

"Yes . . . ? Ah—Todd?" George Orson said, and Toddzilla grinned, showing his large orthodontic teeth.

"So Mr. O," he said. He was one of those teenage jock boys who thought it was cool to call teachers and other adults by trite, jocky nicknames. "So Mr. O," Toddzilla said. "Where'd you get your car? That's an awesome car."

"Oh," George Orson said. "Thank you."

"What make is that? Is that a Maserati?"

"It is." George Orson looked at the rest of them, and Lucy thought that for a fraction of a second she and George Orson had looked directly at each other, that they were in communion, silently agreeing that Toddzilla was a Neanderthal. Then George Orson turned his attention down to his desk, to the syllabus or whatever.

"So, why would you become a high school teacher if you can afford a car like that?" Toddzilla said.

"Well, I guess I just find teaching high school really fulfilling," George Orson said. Straight-faced. He looked again at Lucy, and the corners of his mouth lifted enough so that his dimple peeked out. There was a sharpness, a glint of secret hilarity that perhaps only she could see. Lucy smiled. He was funny, she thought. *Interesting.*

But Todd hadn't liked it. Later, in study hall, in the cafeteria, she heard him repeating the same question, critically. "How can a high school teacher afford a car like that?" Toddzilla wanted to know. "Full-fucking-filling, my ass. I think he's some rich pervert or something. He just likes to be around teenagers."

Which was probably the first time she thought: *Hmmm.* She herself was intrigued by the idea of a wealthy George Orson, his soft but masculine, veiny hands.

They had left Pompey in the Maserati, and maybe that had been the reason she felt so confident. She looked good in that car, she thought, people would look at them as they were cruising down the interstate, a guy in an SUV who watched her as they passed, and he made a display of winking at her, like a silent movie actor or a mime. *Wink.* And she made her own show of not noticing, though in fact she had even bought a tube of bright red lipstick, sort of as a joke, but when she looked at herself in the passenger side mirror, she was privately pleased by the effect.

Who would you be if you weren't Lucy?

Which was a question they found themselves talking about frequently, when George Orson wasn't sequestered in the "study."

Who would you be?

One day, George Orson found an old set of bow and arrows in the garage, and they went down to the beach to try shooting them. He hadn't been able to find an actual target, and so he spent a lot of time setting up various objects for Lucy to shoot arrows at. A pyramid stack of soda cans, for example. An ancient beach ball, which inflated only halfheartedly. A large cardboard box, which he drew circles on with black Magic Marker.

And as Lucy nocked her arrow into the string and drew back the bow, trying to aim, George Orson would ask her questions.

"Would you rather be an unpopular dictator, or a popular president?"

"That's easy," Lucy said.

"Would you rather be poor and live in a beautiful place, or be rich and live in an ugly place?"

"I don't think poor people ever live in beautiful places," she said.

"Would you rather drown, or freeze to death, or die in a fire?"

"George," she said, "why are you always so morbid?" And he smiled tightly.

"Would you want to go to college, even if you had enough money that you'd never have to get a real job?

"Which is to say," George Orson continued. "Do you want to go because you want to be an educated person, or do you only go because you want a career of some sort?"

"Hmm," Lucy said, and tried to draw a bead on the beach ball, which was lolling woozily in the wind. "I think I just want to be an educated person, actually. Though maybe if I had so much money that I never had to work, I'd probably choose a different major. Something impractical."

"I see," George Orson said. He stood behind her; she could feel his chest against her back as he tried to help her take aim. "Like what?" he said.

"Like history," Lucy said, and smiled sidelong at him as she released the arrow, which traveled in a wobbling, uncertain arc before landing in the sand about a foot away from the beach ball.

"You're close!" George Orson whispered—still pressed close up against her, his hand around her waist, his mouth alongside her ear. She could feel the wing-brush of his lips moving. "Very close," he said.

She thought about this again as she went outdoors and stood there in her sleep T-shirt, her hair flattened against the side of her head and nothing attractive about her at all, currently.

"George?" she called—yet again.

And she stepped tenderly barefoot across the gravel driveway toward the garage. It was a wooden barnlike structure with high weeds growing up along the sides of it, and when she drew closer, a flurry of grasshoppers scattered, startled by her approach. Their dry wings made a maraca sound like rattlesnakes; she pulled her hair back into a ponytail and held it with her fist.

They hadn't driven the Maserati since they arrived here. "Too conspicuous," George Orson said. "There's no sense in calling a lot of attention to ourselves," he said, and then the next day she woke and he was already out of bed and he wasn't in the house and she found him at last in the garage.

There were two cars in there. The Maserati was on the left, completely covered by an olive-green tarp. On the right was an old red and white Ford Bronco pickup, possibly from the 1970s or 80s. The hood of the pickup was open and George Orson was leaning into it.

He was wearing an old pair of mechanic's coveralls, and she almost laughed out loud. She couldn't imagine where he had found such an outfit.

"George," she said. "I've been looking all over for you. What are you *doing*?"

"I'm fixing a truck," he said.

"Oh," she said.

And though he was basically still himself, he looked—what?—*costumed* in the dirty coveralls, his hair uncombed and standing up, fingers black with grease, and she felt a twinge.

"I didn't know that you knew how to fix cars," Lucy said, and George Orson gave her a long look. A sad look, she thought, as if he were recalling a mistake he'd made in the distant past.

"There are probably a lot of things you don't know about me," he said.

Which gave her pause, now, as she vacillated at the mouth of the garage.

The truck was gone, and a shiver of unease passed across her as she stared at the bare cement floor, an oil spot in the dust where the old Bronco had been.

He'd gone out—had left her alone—had left her—

The Maserati was still there, still covered in its tarp. She was not completely abandoned.

Though she was aware that she didn't have the key to the Maserati.

And even if she *did* have a key, she didn't know how to drive a stick shift.

She mulled this over, looked at the shelves: oil cans and bottles of nuclear-blue windshield wiper fluid and jars full of screws and bolts and nails and washers.

Nebraska was even worse than Ohio—if such a thing were possible. There was a soundlessness about this place, she thought, though sometimes the wind made the glass in the windowpanes hum, the wind running in a long exhaled stream through the weeds and dust and dry bed of the lake, and sometimes unexpectedly there would be a very startling sonic boom over the house as a military plane broke the sound barrier, and there was the rattle of the grasshoppers leaping from one weed to the next—

But mostly it was silence, a kind of end-of-the-world hush, and you could feel the sky sealing over you like the glass around a snow globe.

She was still in the garage when George Orson returned.

She had pulled back the tarp from the Maserati, and she was sitting in the driver's seat and wishing that she knew how to hot-wire a car. How appropriate, she thought, for George Orson to come back and find his beloved Maserati missing, and it would serve him right, and she liked to imagine the look on his face when she pulled back up the driveway sometime after dark—

She was still fantasizing about this when George Orson drove into the space beside her with the old Bronco. He looked puzzled as he opened the door—why was the tarp off of his Maserati?—but when he saw her sitting there, his expression opened into a gratifying look of alarm.

"Lucy?" he said. He was wearing jeans and a black T-shirt, very nondescript—his version of a native costume—and she had to admit that he didn't look like a wealthy man. He didn't even look like a teacher, with his face unshaved and his hair growing out and his jaw hard with suspicion, he could actually be said to look menacing and middle-aged. Briefly she had a memory of the father of her friend Kayleigh, who was divorced and lived in Youngstown and drank too much, and who had taken them to the Cedar Point amusement park when they were twelve, and she could imagine Kayleigh's father in the parking lot of Cedar Point leaning up against the hood of the car, smoking a cigarette as they came toward him, she remembered being aware of the way his arms were muscled and his eyes were fixed on her, and she thought, *Is he staring at my boobs?*

"Lucy, what are you doing?" George Orson said, and she looked at him hard.

Of course, the real George Orson was still there, underneath, if he cleaned himself up.

"I was just getting ready to drive off in your car and steal it and go to Mexico," Lucy said.

And his face settled back into itself, into the George Orson she knew, the George Orson who loved it when she was sarcastic.

"Sweetie," George Orson said. "I made a quick trip into town, that's all. I had to get some supplies—and I wanted to make you a nice dinner."

"I don't like being ditched," Lucy said sternly.

"You were sleeping," George Orson said. "I didn't want to wake you."

He ran a hand across the back of his hair—yes, he realized it was getting shaggy—and then he reached down and opened the door to the Maserati and climbed into the passenger seat.

"I left a note," he said. "On the kitchen table. I guess you didn't find it."

"No," she said. They were silent, and she couldn't help it, that slow, vacant feeling was opening up inside her chest, that end-of-the-world loneliness, and she put her hands on the steering wheel as if she were driving somewhere.

"I don't appreciate being left alone here," she said.

They looked at each other.

"I'm sorry," George Orson said.

His hand lowered over hers, and she could feel the smooth pressure of his palm against the back of her hand, and he was, after all, possibly the only person left in the world who truly loved her.

9

Back in the days before Hayden began to believe that his phone was being tapped, back when he and Miles were in their early twenties, he used to call fairly frequently. Once a month, sometimes more.

The phone would ring in the middle of the night. Two A.M. Three A.M. "It's me," Hayden would say, though of course who else would it be, at such an hour? "Thank God you finally picked up the phone," he would say. "Miles, you've got to help me, I can't sleep."

Sometimes he would be worked up about an article he had read on psychic phenomena or reincarnation, past lives, spiritualism. The usual.

Sometimes he would start ranting on the subject of their childhood, telling stories about events that Miles had no memory of whatsoever—events he was fairly certain Hayden had invented.

But there was no arguing with him. If Miles expressed any reservation or doubt, Hayden could easily become defensive, belligerent, and then who knew what would happen? The one time they'd gotten into a heated disagreement about his "memories," Hayden had slammed down the phone and hadn't called again for more than two months. Miles was beside himself. Back then, Miles still believed that it was only a matter of time before he tracked Hayden down, only a matter of time before Hayden could be captured or otherwise induced to come home. He had an image of Hayden, calmed and perhaps medicated, the two of them sharing a small apartment, peaceably playing video games after Miles came home from work. Starting a business together. He knew this was ridiculous.

Still, when Hayden resurfaced at last, Miles was very conciliatory. He was so relieved that he told himself he was never going to argue with Hayden again, no matter what Hayden said.

It was four in the morning, and Miles was sitting up in bed, holding the phone tightly, his heart beating fast. "Just tell me where you are, Hayden," he said. "Don't go anywhere."

"Miles, Miles," Hayden said. "I love it that you worry!"

He claimed that he was living in Los Angeles; he had a bungalow, he said, right off Sunset Boulevard in Silver Lake. "You won't find me if you come looking for me," he said, "but if it makes you feel any better, that's where I am."

"I'm relieved," Miles said, and he took out one of the yellow sticky notes he kept on his nightstand and wrote: "Sunset Blvd." and "Silver Lake."

"I'm relieved, too," Hayden said. "You're the only one I can really talk to, you know that, don't you?" Miles listened as Hayden drew an extended breath that he imagined was probably smoke from a joint. "You're the only person in the world who still loves me."

Hayden had been thinking a lot about their childhood—or rather, *his* childhood, since the truth was Miles didn't recall any of the incidents Hayden was obsessing about. But Miles kept his objections to himself. It was the first time Hayden had called him since their argument, and Miles stared down at his little sticky note in silence as Hayden held forth.

"I've been thinking a lot about Mr. Breeze," Hayden was saying. "Do you remember him?"

And Miles wavered. "Well," Miles said, and Hayden made an impatient sound.

"He was that hypnotist, don't you remember?" Hayden said. "He was pretty good friends with Mom and Dad—he was always at those parties back in the day. I think he dated Aunt Helen for a while."

"Uh-huh," Miles said, noncommittally. "And his name was 'Mr. Breeze'?"

"That was probably his stage name," Hayden said. His voice stiffened. "Geez, Miles, you don't remember anything. You never paid attention, you know that?"

"I guess not," Miles said.

Supposedly, according to Hayden, this incident with Mr. Breeze happened at one of the parties their parents used to have. It was late at night, the wee hours, and Hayden came down to the kitchen in his pajamas, couldn't sleep, sweaty from the top bunk, the forced air vent had been blowing from the ceiling onto him, he'd been awake anyway from the sounds of music and laughter and the thick hum of adult talking that came wafting through the floorboards and into his dreams. As for Miles, he would have been peacefully asleep in the bottom bunk. *Insensate*, as always.

The two of them, Miles and Hayden, were eight years old but small for their age, and Hayden was cute and solemn as he drank his glass of water in the kitchen. Mr. Breeze lifted him up and put him on a stool at the counter.

"Tell me, little boy," Mr. Breeze said, in his deep, deep voice. "Do you know what 'cryptomnesia' means?"

Mr. Breeze looked down into Hayden's eyes as if he were admiring his own reflection in a pool, and he took his index finger and let it hover right at the center of Hayden's forehead, though he didn't let it touch.

"Do you ever remember things that didn't really happen to you?" Mr. Breeze said.

"No," Hayden said. He looked, unsmiling, back at Mr. Breeze, in the way he always looked adults in the eye: impertinent. Their aunt Helen had come in and she stayed, watching.

"Portis," she said. "Don't tease that child."

"I'm not," Mr. Breeze said. He was dressed in black jeans and a flowered cowboy shirt, and he had lines around his mouth that looked as if someone had ironed creases there. He peered kindly at Hayden's face.

"You're not afraid, are you, young man?" Mr. Breeze said. Out in the next room, there was the sound of the party, some bluesy rock song, some people slow-dancing; out in the yard, a drunk lady wept bitterly while a drunken friend tried to counsel her.

"We're just going to take a wee peek at his past lives," Mr. Breeze told Aunt Helen. And he beamed at Hayden. "What do you think about that, Hayden? All the people that you used to be, once upon a time!" Mr. Breeze drew in a soft, anticipatory breath, barely audible.

"I so seldom get a chance to work with a child," he said.

This Mr. Breeze was fiercely drunk, Miles imagined. So was Aunt Helen, probably. So were all the other adults in the house.

But even drunk Mr. Breeze held Hayden pinned fast with only the pupils of his eyes. "You want to be hypnotized, don't you, Hayden?" he said.

Hayden's lips parted, and his tongue tingled in his mouth.

"Yes," Hayden heard himself say.

The gaze of Mr. Breeze locked into Hayden like one puzzle piece fits into another.

"I want you to tell me what it was like when you died," Mr. Breeze said. "That moment," he said. "Tell me about that moment."

———

Mr. Breeze had taken Hayden and slit him open the way a fisherman would slit open the belly of a trout. That was what Hayden said. "Not my physical body," Hayden explained. "It was my spirit. Whatever you want to call it. My soul. You know. Inner self."

"What do you mean by 'slit' you open," Miles said uneasily. "I don't get it."

"I'm not saying sexual," Hayden said. "You always assume sexual, Miles, you pervert."

Miles shifted the phone where it was making an uncomfortable, sweaty spot against his ear. It was getting close to five in the morning.

"So—?" Miles said.

"So that was how it started," Hayden said. "Mr. Breeze told me I had more past lives than any other person he'd ever met—"

"*A harvest,*" Mr. Breeze told Hayden. "You produce an unusually large harvest," he said. The lives were clustered inside of Hayden like roe—

"Fish eggs," Hayden said. "That's what 'roe' means."

"Yes, I *know,*" Miles said, and Hayden sighed.

"The thing is, Miles," Hayden said, "no one realizes, once these things have been opened up, you can't close them again. That's what I'm trying to explain to you. If most people had to live with the memories I've had to live with, a lot of them would kill themselves."

"You mean your nightmares," Miles said.

"Yes," he said. "That's how we used to refer to them. I know better now."

"Like the pirate stuff," Miles said.

"*Pirate stuff,*" Hayden said, and then he was witheringly silent. "You make it sound like some little romp through Neverland."

The pirate stuff, so-called, had been one of the recurring nightmares of Hayden's childhood, but they hadn't talked about it in years. It was true that he used to wake up screaming. Horrible, horrible screams. Miles could still hear them vividly.

In the dream Hayden used to talk about, he was a boy on a pirate ship. A cabin boy, Miles supposed. Hayden remembered a coil of heavy rope where he would curl up to sleep. There was the dense flapping of the sails and the creak of the masts as he lay there trying to rest, and the smell of wet wood and barnacles, and when he opened his eyes a crack, he would see the bare dirty feet of the pirates, which always had infected sores on them. He would huddle there, hoping not to be noticed, because sometimes the pirates would give him a kick. Sometimes they would grab him by the back of his shirt or his hair and yank him onto his feet.

"They always want me to kiss them," Hayden would tell Miles. This was back when he was eight, ten years old, and he had woken up screaming. "They always want me to kiss them on the lips." He grimaced: their breath, their nasty teeth, the filth in their beards.

"Gross," Miles said. And he remembered thinking even then that there was an unnatural quality to Hayden's dreams. The pirates would kiss Hayden, and sometimes they would cut off a hank of hair—"as a reminder of yer kisses, me lad"—and one of them even cut off a piece of his earlobe.

This particular pirate was Bill McGregor, and he was the one Hayden feared the most. Bill McGregor was the worst of them—and at night when everyone else was asleep, Bill McGregor would come looking for Hayden, his step slow and hollow on the planks of the deck, his voice a deep whisper.

"Boy," he would murmur. "Where are you, boy?"

After Bill McGregor cut off the piece of Hayden's earlobe, he decided that he wanted more. Every time he caught Hayden, he would cut a small piece off of him. The skin of an elbow, the tip of a finger, a piece of his lip. He would grip the squirming Hayden and cut a piece off of him, and then Bill McGregor would eat the piece of flesh.

"And when I'm finished playing with ye," Bill McGregor whispered, "I'm going to sneak up behind you and—"

Which is exactly what he did, according to Hayden. It was a spring night and Bill McGregor came up from behind him and clapped his hands tightly over Hayden's eyes and slit his throat and tossed him overboard, and Hayden went flailing into the sea with his neck clutched between his hands as if he were trying to throttle himself, blood gurgling out between his fingers. He could see a trickle of blood droplets falling upward as he plunged headfirst into the ocean—he was aware of the moon and the starry sky vanishing beneath his feet, the swallowing sound he made when he hit the water, the fish flitting away as he sank deeper, strands of seaweed, unfurling eddies of jugular blood, his mouth opening and closing, limbs growing limp.

His exact moment of death.

Yes, of course Miles knew about this. Hayden had the dream regularly when they were kids, once or twice a week sometimes. He would jump down into the bottom bunk and under the covers with Miles—and if Miles wasn't awake yet, he would shake him until he was. "Miles," he would say. "Miles! Nightmares! Oh, God! Nightmares!" And he would curl up around Miles as if they were back together in their mother's belly.

Miles had always prided himself on the fact that he was a good brother. He never got angry, no matter how many times he heard the story of Bill McGregor and so on.

But when he mentioned something to that effect, Hayden didn't speak for a long time.

"Oh, *right*," Hayden said. "You were such a good brother to me."

They sat there listening to each other breathing. On Hayden's end, there was the gurgling sound of a bong. Not surprising.

Yes, Miles knew what he was getting at. Hayden thought that he should have stuck by him no matter what. He thought that Miles should have just thrown away his relationship with their mother and the rest of the family and sided with him, no matter how extreme his stories and quarrels and accusations became.

This wasn't a topic that Miles felt comfortable discussing, but with Hayden it was difficult to avoid. Sooner or later, every conversation would circle back to these various obsessions that he had, his nightmares, his memories, his grudges against their family—

"His pathological lies," their mother called them. "He is a deeply, deeply troubled person, Miles," she said, on any number of occasions. She used to warn him that he was too easily deceived, that he was too much Hayden's follower—"his little factotum," she said, acidly.

This was during that period when she was trying to get Hayden institutionalized and she said, "Just you wait, Miles, sweetheart, because someday he will betray you just like he has betrayed everyone else. It's only a matter of time."

And so when Hayden called and said that he needed help, he needed his brother's help—"Just to talk awhile, I can't sleep, Miles, please just talk to me"—well, Miles couldn't keep from thinking of his mother's warning.

It was especially difficult when Hayden would insist so strongly on his version of their lives, his version of events. Events that Miles was pretty certain had never actually happened.

"The thing I'm confused about," Miles told Hayden—they had been talking now for hours about past lives and pirates, and even though Miles was exhausted, he was trying to be good-natured and reasonable. "I'm a little puzzled," Miles said, "about this guy. Mr. Breeze. Because I honestly don't remember you ever telling me anything about him before, and it seems like you would've."

"Oh, I told you about him," Hayden said. "Most definitely."

This was a few weeks after he had begun to obsess about the whole "hypnotist in the kitchen" story. Miles was at a rest area off of the interstate, with his window rolled down, talking on a drive-up pay phone. It was probably about two in the morning. A map of the United States was spread out across the steering wheel.

Hayden was saying, ". . . maybe the problem is that you *repressed* so much about our childhood. Do you ever consider that?"

"Well," Miles said. He took a sip from a bottle of water.

"It's not as if this hasn't been an ongoing ordeal in my life," Hayden said. "Remember Bobby Berman? Remember Amos Murley?"

"Yes," Miles said—and it was true, these were familiar names from their childhood, familiar people from Hayden's nightmares. Bobby Berman was the boy who liked to play with matches, and who had burned to death in a toolshed behind his house; Amos Murley was the teenager who had been drafted into the Union Army during the Civil War, the one who died while dragging himself across a battlefield, his legs blown off below the knee. Their mother used to call them Hayden's "imaginary characters."

"Oh, Hayden," she would say, with exasperation. "Why can't you make up stories about *happy* people? Why does everything have to be so morbid?"

And Hayden would blush, shrugging resentfully. He said nothing. It wasn't until much later that Hayden began to claim these were his own past lives he was dreaming about. That these "characters" were, in fact, people he had actually *been*. That the terrible life he was leading with their family was just one of many terrible lives he had led.

But it wasn't until their father died that Hayden had begun to understand the true nature of his affliction.

At least, that was the version of events he was currently espousing. It wasn't until their father was gone and their mother had remarried and the hateful Marc Spady was living with them in their house. Only then did he begin to grasp the extent of what Mr. Breeze had "opened up" inside him.

"That's the thing I wasn't prepared for, you see," Hayden said. "I came to realize that it wasn't just me—*it was everyone.*"

Steadily, he had begun to comprehend, Hayden said. He had become aware that he was not the only person who had these past lives. *Obviously not!* Little by little, in crowds, in restaurants, in faces glimpsed on television, in small gestures of schoolmates and relatives—little by little he had begun to feel vague glimmerings of recognition. An eye, shifting sidelong—the fingers of a cashier, brushing his palm—the discolored front tooth of their geometry teacher—the voice of their stepfather, Marc Spady, which was, Hayden said, the exact gravelly voice of the pirate Bill McGregor.

When their father died, Hayden began to see connections in every face. Where had he come across that one before? In what life? No doubt nearly every soul had encountered the others in one permutation or another, all of them interconnected, entangled, their pathways crisscrossing backward into prehistory, into space and infinity like some terrible mathematical formula.

Clearly it had to do with their father's death, Miles thought. Before that, Hayden was just an overimaginative boy who had nightmares, and Mr. Breeze, if he existed, was just another of their father's unusual acquaintances, drunk at a party.

"Oh, spare me," Hayden said, when Miles tried to suggest this. "How facile!" he said. "Is that what *Mom* told you? That I became a so-called schizophrenic because I couldn't handle Dad's death? I know you don't like me to cast aspersions on your intelligence, but *really*. That's so completely simpleminded."

"Well," Miles said. He didn't want to get into an argument about it, but it had been evident that Hayden had undergone some private transformation in the months following their father's death. That was when they were thirteen, a year after they had started working on the atlas together, and Hayden grew moodier and moodier, angrier, more withdrawn. It had seemed to Miles that Hayden was more susceptible to certain kinds of mementos and reminders of the dead—all the insignificant objects everywhere in the house, now glowing with their father's absence, which Hayden had begun to accumulate. Here: a gum wrapper that their father had distractedly folded into an origami bird and left on his dresser among some loose change. Here: a pencil with his tooth marks, an unmatched sock, an appointment card from the dentist.

His voice on the answering machine, which they'd forgotten to change until one day Hayden called home and their father's voice answered after the phone rang and rang:

"Hello. You've reached the Cheshire residence . . ."

Which was plainly a recording; you could tell after only a second.

But for that second! For that second, a person's heart might leap up, a person might imagine that it had all been a bad dream, that some miracle had happened.

"Dad?" Hayden said, catching his breath.

He and Miles were at the skating rink in the rec center, calling for their mother to come and pick them up, and Miles stood beside Hayden as he spoke into the pay phone.

"Dad?" And Miles could see the brief light of supernatural hopefulness flicker across Hayden's face before it closed down, a light of surprised joy that shrank almost immediately as it dawned on him: he had been fooled. Their father was still dead, more dead than he had been before.

Miles could sense all this, all this passed through Miles's mind as if by telepathy, he experienced Hayden's emotions in the old way that he used to when they were little, when Miles would cry out in pain when Hayden's finger was slammed in a door, when Miles would laugh at a joke before Hayden even told it, when he knew the look on Hayden's face even when they weren't in the same room.

But things weren't like that anymore.

Hayden's expression pinched—he glared abruptly, as if Miles's empathy were a disgusting, groping touch. As if, having witnessed Hayden's display of naked eagerness, Miles ought now to be punished. "Shut up, moron," Hayden said, even though Miles had said nothing, and Hayden turned away, not even willing to look Miles in the eye.

Resolved: never to be happy again.

Was it naïve to think that before their father died they had all been pretty content? Miles had thought about this as he drove down the interstate, as he passed through Illinois, Iowa, Nebraska—Los Angeles still thousands of miles distant.

Things had been nice, Miles thought. *Hadn't they?*

When they were growing up, Cleveland was fairly idyllic, to Miles at least. This was where their parents had settled early in their marriage, on the east side of town, a comfortable old three-story house on a street lined with big silver maples. It was a pleasantly run-down middle-class neighborhood, a little to the north of the mansions on Fairmount Boulevard, a little to the south of the slums on the other side of Mayfield Road, and Miles remembered thinking that this wasn't such a bad position to be in. Growing up, he and Hayden had friends who were both appreciably poorer and appreciably richer than they, and their father told them that they should pay attention to the homes and families of their peers. "Learn what it is like in another life," he said. "Think hard about it, boys. People *choose* their lives; that's what I want you to remember. And what life will you choose for yourselves?"

It was clear that their father himself had thought frequently about this question. He was the proprietor of what he called a "talent agency," though in fact he was all of the employees. Sometimes he worked at children's birthday parties and the grand openings of shopping malls as Periwinkle Clown, making balloon animals and juggling and face-painting and leading sing-alongs and so forth. Sometimes he was the Amazing Cheshire, a magician. ("Amaze Your Clients and Guests with Magical Fun! Trade Shows! Corporate Events! Special Occasions!") Still other times he was known as Dr.

Larry Cheshire, certified hypnotist, smoking-cessation specialist, and motivational speaker; or Lawrence Cheshire, Ph.D., hypno-therapist.

Miles and Hayden had never in their lives seen him perform as any of these characters, though they would occasionally come across photos of him in his various guises laying around the house, even snippets of promotional material he was working on: "Peri-winkle Clown and his puppet friends invite you to a magical hour of storytelling . . ." or "Cheshire Hypnotics Workshops will help you discover the powers of your own mind . . ."

Occasionally, they would hear him on the phone, sitting at the kitchen table with his large black appointment book, pausing to bite thoughtfully on his pencil. They found it hilarious that he would take on different voices depending on whom he was talking to. An earnest, boyish dopiness when he was Periwinkle; a sleek managerial smoothness when he was Dr. Larry Cheshire; a baritone stage-trained plumminess when he was speaking for the Amazing Cheshire; a somewhat affectless, calming monotone when he was Lawrence Cheshire, Ph.D.

They would hear such stuff, but it felt disconnected from the man they knew, who was so utterly unlike the various costumed folks in makeup and hats and toupees that he wore over the bald head they were used to at home. Miles didn't remember him doing anything that could have been identified as "theatrical," and in fact he was perhaps even unusually subdued and wistful in his everyday life. Miles supposed it was simply that when he came home from work, he was tired of performing for people.

But he was a good dad, nevertheless. Attentive in his restrained way.

They played cards together, Miles and Hayden and their father, board games, computer games. They went camping a few times, and on nature walks. When they were small, Miles and Hayden were particularly fond of the world of insects, which their father would help them find by turning over large rocks and logs. Identifying the creatures, reciting from his paperback Peterson guide.

He liked to read aloud. *Goodnight Moon* was the first book Miles recalled. *The Return of the King* was the last, finished only a week or so before their father's death.

Even though they were almost thirteen, they liked to sleep next to him when he took his afternoon naps. The three of them, Miles and Hayden and their father, lined up on the king-size bed in their stocking feet, Hayden on one side, Miles on the other, the dog nestled down at the foot of the bed, curled up with her muzzle resting on her tail. Their mother had photographs of them all sleeping this way. Sometimes she would just stand in the doorway, watching. She loved how peaceful they all were, she said. Her boys. She might've been a good mother, Miles thought, if their father had lived.

Their father had been fifty-three years old when he died. It was completely unexpected, of course, though as it turned out his blood pressure had been extremely high and he hadn't been taking care of his body very well. He had been a regular, if secretive, smoker, and he was overweight and hadn't bothered to watch what he ate. "Cholesterol through the roof," their mother had murmured to people at the funeral, and Miles could sense that she was making her way through thickets, mazes of regret and possible preventative measures that might have been taken, and alternate futures, now fruitless but still occupying her thoughts. "I told him I was concerned," she said to people, earnestly, urgently, as if she expected them to blame her. "I spoke to him about it."

In the weeks that followed, Miles spent a lot of time thinking about this. His death. Had they failed his father, had they been inattentive, could they have acted in a way that might have changed the course of events? He would close his eyes and try to imagine what a "massive heart attack" would feel like. Did you just go blank, he wondered, did your mind just empty out, like water spilled out of a cup?

He tried to picture what it might have been like, tried to picture his father standing in front of the audience when the first twinges came upon him. A pain in his left arm, maybe. A tightening in his chest. *Heartburn*, he probably thought. *Exhaustion*. Miles imagined him putting his hands against his toupee, pressing it down tightly with both palms.

Miles thought he knew the basic facts of what had happened. He remembered talking to Hayden about it on the night their father had died.

Their father had been out of town for a weekend event in Indianapolis and he'd died during one of his hypnotism shows.

It would have made a cute news item, Hayden said. One of those jokey, heavily ironic human interest pieces you might read about in *News of the Weird*.

The performance was taking place in a conference room in an office complex on the outskirts of the city; it was a "team-building" exercise for the people in the company, probably some bright idea that a manager in human resources had. *Neat!* they thought. Their father probably convinced them with a pitch about "helping people discover the power of their own mind," and he took volunteers from among the group, people who were bravely willing to be hypnotized, and he brought them up to the front of the room and had them sit down in folding chairs while their coworkers watched, and everyone waited expectantly as one by one their father put each of the volunteers into their own individual trances.

Everyone was delighted. What fun! The coworkers in the audience were tittering to see their colleagues actually hypnotized, deeply relaxed, deeply vulnerable, right there in chairs in front of everyone.

Their father was perspiring a little as he spoke. He pressed the palm of his hand against his forehead, then the back of his neck.

"Ladies and gentlemen," he said, and swallowed a dryness in his throat.

"Ladies and

"Ladies and gen   tlemen."

And then they were all hushed as he raised a finger—*one moment please,* the gesture meant—and then he sat down on a folding chair beside the hypnotized volunteers. The audience chuckled. The last guy in the row was a goofy curly-haired computer dude, slack-jawed, and they were particularly amused by him, he was in such a deep trance.

They waited to see what would happen. Their father put his hand on his chin and appeared to be thinking. He squeezed his eyes shut in a posture of solemn contemplation.

More chuckling.

Probably he died about then.

Sitting in a folding chair—his body balanced, equilibrated, and his audience was still waiting.

A few more chuckles, but mostly expectant silence. A held breath.

Their father's body slumped slightly. Then tilted. Then—at last—fell over, and the metal chair folded shut with a metallic clap onto the echoing tile floor.

A lady cried out in surprise, but still the audience continued to sit there, uncertain, uncertain. Was this part of the act? Was it part of the team-building?

And meanwhile the people who had been hypnotized were not hypnotized any longer. It was, after all, not possible to become stuck in a trance. That is just a myth.

The hypnotized volunteers had begun to stir, to open their eyes and peek out.

Wake up! Wake up! Miles and Hayden's father used to call out in the mornings when they were young. *Wake, my little sleepyheads,* he would whisper, and he would touch their ears lightly with the soft tips of his fingers.

In truth, this was not an event any of them—Miles or Hayden or their mother—had actually witnessed, but in Miles's mind's eye it was always as if he'd actually watched it. As if it had been filmed, one of those grainy, boxy educational movies the teachers would dust off on a rainy day at Roxboro Middle School. *Martin Luther King. The Reproductive System. Mummies in Egypt.*

Sometime later, Miles happened to mention this scene, this scene of their father's death, and his mother had studied him.

"Miles, what on earth are you talking about?" she said. She was sitting at the kitchen table, very still, though her cigarette was shaking between her fingers. "Is that what Hayden told you?" she said, and she regarded him worriedly. Her feelings about Hayden were beginning to solidify.

"Your father died in his hotel room, honey," she said. "A maid found him. He was staying at a Holiday Inn. And it was in Minneapolis, not Indianapolis, if you want to know, and he was attending the convention of the National Guild of Hypnotists. He wasn't performing."

She took a sip from her coffee, then lifted her head sharply as Hayden came into the kitchen in his boxer shorts and T-shirt, just waking up though it was two in the afternoon.

"Well, well," she said. "Speak of the devil."

Even then, Miles had begun to realize that many of his "memories" were simply stories that Hayden had told him—suggestions that had been planted, seeds around which his brain had begun to build "setting" and "detail" and "action." Even years later, Miles remembered his father's last moments most vividly in the version that Hayden had described.

Looking back, it was as if there had been two different lives that Miles was leading—one narrated by Hayden, the other the life he was living separately, the life of a more or less normal teenager. While Hayden was delving deeper into the world of the past lives that Mr. Breeze had opened up, while Hayden was becoming more and more isolated, Miles was working on the high school yearbook and playing lacrosse on the junior varsity team at Hawken School, where Marc Spady was director of admissions. While Hayden was going into therapy and staying up all hours of the night, Miles was placidly getting B's and C's in his classes and going out to practice for his driving test with Marc Spady, backing through orange cones in a parking lot while Spady stood a few yards from the car calling: "Careful, Miles! Careful!"

Meanwhile, Hayden's life was moving in a different direction. His nightmares had grown more and more pronounced—pirates and bloody Civil War battles and that burning shed where Bobby Berman had been playing with matches, where the flames sucked the oxygen from his lungs—and this meant that Hayden rarely slept. Their mother made up a new bedroom for him in the attic, and a special bed with cloth straps for his wrists and ankles just to keep him from sleepwalking, or from hurting himself in his sleep. There had been the night that he busted the kitchen windows with the ham of his palms, blood everywhere. There had been the time that their mother and Marc Spady woke to find him standing over them with a hammer, wavering there, mumbling to himself.

And so it was for his own safety, for all their safeties, it wasn't a punishment, but Miles had been surprised at how willingly Hayden had accepted this new arrangement. "Don't worry about me, Miles," Hayden had said, though Miles wasn't sure what, exactly, he was supposed to be worried about. Hayden got video games, cable TV in his new room, and in fact Miles used to be a little jealous of this. He remembered evenings when they would lie there in Hayden's attic room, in bed together, playing Super Mario on that old Nintendo system, side by side holding their game pads and staring at the miniature TV screen on Hayden's dresser. "Don't worry, Miles," Hayden said. "I'm taking care of everything."

"That's good," Miles said.

Hayden had already been through "a battery" of psychologists and therapists, as their mother said. Various prescriptions. Olanzapine, haloperidol. But it didn't matter, Hayden said.

"It's not like I can tell anyone the truth," Hayden said, and the MIDI music of Super Mario was burbling along. "You're the only one I can talk to, Miles," he said.

"Uh-huh," Miles said, mostly focused on the journey of his Mario across the screen. They were sitting there under the covers together, and Hayden slid over and stuck his ice-cold foot against Miles's leg. Hayden's hands and feet were always pale and freezing, bad circulation, and he was always sticking them under Miles's clothes.

"Cut it out!" Miles said, and in the game a mushroom monster killed him. "Oh, man! Look what you made me do!"

But Hayden just gazed at him. "Pay attention, Miles," he said, and Miles watched as the GAME OVER tablet came up onto the TV screen.

"What?" Miles said, and their eyes caught. That significant look, as if, Miles thought, as if he should *know*.

"I told them about Marc Spady," Hayden said, and let out a soft breath. "I told them who Spady *was*, and what he did to us."

"What are you talking about?" Miles said, and then Hayden looked up abruptly. Their mother was standing in the doorway. It was time for them to go to bed, and she had come to strap Hayden in.

Miles had arrived at last in California. This was the first time he had known Hayden's location in quite a while. More than four years had passed. Miles didn't even know what Hayden looked like, though since they were twins, he imagined that they still looked a lot alike, of course.

This was in late June, just after they had turned twenty-two, and their mother and Marc Spady were dead, and Miles had been roaming from job to job ever since he dropped out of college. He came to the end of I-70 in the middle of Utah, then followed I-15 south toward Las Vegas.

When he came at last to the edge of Los Angeles, it was morning.

There was a Super 8 motel near Chinatown, and he slept the whole day on the thin-mattressed bed in his room, curtains closed tightly against the California sunshine, listening to the hum of the miniature refrigerator. It was after dark when he woke, and he groped around on the nightstand and found his car keys and the alarm clock and, at last, the phone.

"Hello?" Hayden said. It was hard to believe that he was only a few miles away. Miles had traced the path he would take to get to the neighborhood where he lived—up past Elysian Park toward the Silver Lake Reservoir.

"Hello?" Hayden said. "Miles?" And Miles deliberated.

"Yes," he said. "It's me."

10

An invader arrives in your computer and begins to glean the little diatoms of your identity.

Your name, your address, and so on; the various websites you visit as you wander through the Internet, your user names and passwords, your birth date, your mother's maiden name, favorite color, the blogs and news sites you read, the items you shop for, the credit card numbers you enter into the databases—

Which isn't necessarily *you*, of course. You are still an individual human being with a soul and a history, friends and relatives and coworkers who care about you, who can vouch for you: they recognize your face and your voice and your personality, and you are aware of your life as a continuous thread, a dependable unfolding story of yourself that you are telling to yourself, you wake up and feel fairly happy—*happy* in that bland, daily way that doesn't even recognize itself as happiness, moving into the empty hours that probably won't be anything more than a series of rote actions: showering and pouring coffee into a cup and dressing and turning a key in the ignition and driving down streets that are so familiar you don't even recall making certain turns and stops—though, yes, you are still *present*, your mind must have consciously carried out the procedure of braking at the corner and rolling the steering wheel beneath your palms and making a left onto the highway even though there is no memory at all of these actions. Perhaps if you were hypnotized such mundane moments could be retrieved, they are written on some file and stored, unused and useless in some neurological clerk's back room. Does it matter? You are still you, after all, through all of these hours and days; you are still whole—

But imagine yourself in pieces.

Imagine all the people who have known you for only a year or a month or a single encounter, imagine those people in a room together trying to assemble a portrait of you, the way an archaeologist puts together the fragments of a ruined façade, or the bones of a caveman. Do you remember the fable of the seven blind men and the elephant?

It's not that easy, after all, to know what you're made up of.

Imagine the parts of yourself disassembled; imagine, for example, that nothing is left of you but a severed hand in an ice cooler. Perhaps there is one of your loved ones who could identify even this small piece. Here: the lines on your palm. The texture of your knuckles and wrinkled skin at the joints in the middle of your fingers. Calluses, scars. The shape of your nails.

Meanwhile, the invaders are busily carrying away small pieces of you, tidbits of information you hardly think about, any more than you think about the flakes of skin that are drifting off of you constantly, any more than you think of the millions of microscopic demodex mites that are crawling over you and feeding off your oil and skin cells.

You don't feel particularly vulnerable, with your firewall and constantly updating virus protection, and most of the predators are almost laughably clumsy. At work you receive an email that is so patently ridiculous that you forward it to a few of your friends. *Miss Emmanuela Kunta, Await Your Reply,* it says in the subject line, and there is something almost adorable about its awkwardness. "Dear One," says Miss Emmanuela Kunta,

Dear One,

I know that this mail will come to you as a surprise since we did not know each other, but I believed that is the will of God for us to know ourselves today and I thank him for making it possible for me to inform you of my great desire of going into long time relationship and financial transaction for our mutual benefits.

Emmanuela Kunta is my name, residing in Abidjan, while I'm 19 years of age, I'm also the only daughter of the late Mr. and Mrs.Godwin Kunta, with my younger brother Emmanuel Kunta who is also 19 years because we are twins.

My father was Gold Agents in Abidjan(Ivory Coast).Before his sudden,death on 20th February in a private hospital here in Abidjan, he called me on his bedside and told me about the sum of (USD $20.000,000,00)Twenty Million United state Dollars, he deposited in a security company here in Abidjan (Ivoiry Coast) for business investment that he used my name his beloved duaghter and only son as the next of kin in depositing the money, because our mother died 13 years ago in a fatal car accident. And that we should seek for a foreign partnerin in any country of our choice where we will transfer this money for investment purpose for our future life.

I humbly seek for your assistance,to help us transfer and secure this money in your country for investment,and to serve as guardian of the fund since we are still students, to make arrangement for us to come over to your country to further our education.Thanks as you made up

your mind to help orphans like us. I am offering you 20% of the total
amount for your humble assistnace and 5% is mapped out to refund
any expenses incure during the transaction.

 Please, I urge you to make this transaction a confidetiallity within
your heart for security purposes. and please reply through my private
email.

 Yours sincerely,
 Miss Emmanuela Kunta

And it's pretty funny. Miss Emmanuela Kunta is probably some
fat thirty-year-old white guy sitting in his mother's basement sur-
rounded by grimy computer equipment, phishing for a sucker.
"Who falls for this?" you would like to know, and your coworkers all
have anecdotes about the scams they have heard of, and the conversation meanders along for a while—it is almost five o'clock—

But for some reason, driving home, you find yourself thinking of
her. Miss Emmanuela Kunta in Abidjan, Côte d'Ivoire, the orphan
daughter of a wealthy gold agent, and she walks along a market
street, the crowds of people and beautiful displays of fruit, a large
blue bowl stacked with papayas and a man in a pink shirt calls after
her—and she turns and her brown eyes are heavy with sorrow.
Await your reply.

Here in upstate New York, it is beginning to snow. You pull off the
interstate and into the forecourt of a gas station and at the pump you
insert your credit card and there is a pause (*One moment please*) while
your card is authorized and then you are approved and you may
begin to dispense fuel. A thick flurry of snowflakes blows across you
as you insert the nozzle into your gas tank, and it is pleasant to think
of the glittering lights of the hotels and the cars passing on the highway that runs along the edge of the Ébrié Lagoon, which Abidjan en-
circles, the palm trees against the indigo sky, etc. *Await your reply.*

———

And meanwhile in another state perhaps a new version of you has already begun to be assembled, someone is using your name and your numbers, a piece of yourself dispersed and dispersing—

And you wipe the snow out of your hair and get back into your car and drive off toward an accumulation of the usual daily stuff—there is dinner to be made and laundry to be done and helping the kids with their homework and watching television on the couch with the dog resting her muzzle in your lap and a phone call you owe to your sister in Wisconsin and getting ready for bed, brushing and flossing and a few different pills that help to regulate your blood pressure and thyroid and a facial scrub that you apply and all the rituals that are—you are increasingly aware—units of measurement by which you are parceling out your life.

PART TWO

✦

Whatever his secret was, I have learnt one secret too, and namely: that the soul is but a manner of being—not a constant state—that any soul may be yours, if you find and follow its undulations. The hereafter may be the full ability of consciously living in any chosen soul, in any number of souls, all of them unconscious of their interchangeable burden.

—VLADIMIR NABOKOV,
The Real Life of Sebastian Knight

11

Ryan had just gotten back from his trip to Milwaukee when the news came that he was deceased.

Drowned, that was what they were saying.

Friends said Schuyler, a scholarship student, was despondent over poor grades, and police now speculate that

Jay sat on the couch, chopping up a bud of dried marijuana, separating out the seeds, as Ryan read the obituary.

"It's interesting, you know?" Jay said. He was already stoned, in a musing mode as he crouched over the coffee table. He had an old-fashioned Ouija board that he used as a surface for cutting up his marijuana, and Ryan stared down at it—the alphabet laid out in the middle, and the sun and moon at the corners—as if there might be a message waiting for him.

"It's like one of those things that practically everybody fantasizes about, right? *What if you woke up one morning and people thought you were dead?* A classic scenario, right? What would you do if you could totally leave your old self behind? That's one of the great mysteries of adulthood. For most people. "

"Mm," Ryan said, and he lowered the printout that Jay had given him. The obituary. He folded it in half and then, uncertain what to do, slipped it into his pocket.

"It's not that easy to accomplish, you know," Jay was saying. "Actually, it's kind of hard to get yourself officially declared dead."

"Uh-huh," Ryan said, and Jay squinted up at him.

"Believe me, Son," Jay said. "I've looked into it, and it's not simple. Especially these days, with DNA tests and dental records and all that. It's a pretty complicated trick to pull off, truth be told—and here you are, you just slipped into it. Smooth as a feather."

"Huh," Ryan said, but he wasn't sure what to say. Jay sat there, leaned back in his sweats and fleece slip-on shoes, peering up at him expectantly.

It was a lot to take in.

He didn't quite see how they could make such a declaration without an actual body, but apparently, according to the newspaper account, a witness had come forward who claimed to have seen him on the rocks on the shore of the lake, just beyond the student center. The witness claimed they had seen him dive into the lake—a young male of his general description, standing on the big graffiti-covered boulders that lined the shore, and then abruptly jumping—

Which, Ryan thought, sounded highly unlikely, easily contradicted. But apparently the police had decided that this was what had happened, apparently they were eager to wrap things up and move on to more important cases.

And so now, he imagined, his parents were on their way to Evanston for the "memorial service," and he guessed that maybe a couple of his friends from high school might also come. Probably quite a few people from his dorm—Walcott, obviously, and some of the other people on his floor he had hung out with, possibly some acquaintances from freshman year he hadn't seen recently. Some teachers. Some of the various administrative people, deans or assistant deans or whatever, functionaries whose job it was to show up and look regretful.

Jay himself—"Uncle Jay"—would not be in attendance, needless to say.

"Honestly, I'm glad your mother doesn't know how to get ahold of me," Jay said. "She'd probably feel compelled to call me, at this point. After all these years, she'd finally want to make peace. She'd probably even ask me to come to the funeral. Jesus! Can you picture it? I haven't laid eyes on her since you were born, man. I can't even imagine the look on her face if I showed up after all these years. That's definitely not something she needs right now, with all she's dealing with."

"Right," Ryan said.

He himself was trying not to imagine the look on his mother's face.

He was trying not to picture the expressions of his parents as they arrived at last in Chicago and checked into their hotel room and dressed in their somber clothes for the memorial. He compressed that image and tamped it down deep in the back of his mind.

"Dude," Jay said. "Why don't you sit down, man? You're concerning me."

They were on the porch of Jay's cabin, and the cast-iron woodstove was sending out waves of sleepy heat, and Jay gazed up from the old porch couch, pushing his bangs back from his eyes. He gave Ryan a wary, compassionate look—the look you give people when you've told them a difficult or tragic fact—but it was not a gaze Ryan wanted to meet.

"You're upset," Jay said. "You're pretending not to be, but I can tell."

"Hm," Ryan said. And he reflected. *Upset?*

"Not exactly," Ryan said. "It's just—it's a lot to try to wrap your mind around."

"No doubt," said Jay, and when Ryan finally sat down beside him, he lowered his arm over Ryan's shoulder. His grip was surprisingly fierce, and he pulled Ryan close with a hug like a wrestler's grapple, pinning Ryan's arms. It was uncomfortable at first, but there was also a degree of comfort in the weight and strength of that arm. He would have been a good dad to have when you were a kid, Ryan thought, and he experimentally rested his head against Jay's shoulder. Just for a second. He was shuddering a little, and Jay squeezed harder.

"Undoubtedly it's going to take some time to sink in," Jay said gently. "This is a pretty huge thing, isn't it?"

"I guess so," Ryan said.

"I mean," Jay said, "look. You have to realize—at the psychological level, this is a loss. This is a death. And you may not think so, but you probably have to, like, process it in the way you would with a real death. Like those Kübler-Ross stages of grief. Denial, anger, bargaining, depression . . . You have to work through a lot of emotions."

"Yeah," Ryan said.

He wasn't entirely sure of what emotion he was currently experiencing. What stage. He watched as Jay fished a beer out of the Styrofoam cooler at their feet. He took the can when Jay handed it to him. He popped the tab, and Jay observed as he tilted the liquid into his mouth.

"But you're not freaking out or anything," Jay said, after they sat there for a while. "You're okay, right?"

"Yeah," Ryan said.

Ryan sat there staring at the old Ouija board on the coffee table. The letters of the alphabet spread out on it like on some old-fashioned keyboard. Smiling sun in the left corner. Frowning moon in the right. In the bottom corners were clouds, and he hadn't noticed this before but inside the clouds were faces. Featureless, indistinct, but, he guessed, slowly emerging from whatever beyond-place there was. Waiting, off to the side, for someone to call them forth.

"You know I'm here for you," Jay said. "I am your father after all. If you want to talk."

"I know," Ryan said.

They drank a few more beers, and then passed a bong back and forth between them, and after a while Ryan began to feel the concept slowly sinking in. He was dead. He had left his old self behind. He put his mouth against the chimney of the bong as Jay lit the bowl. The realization opened up in slow motion, like one of those time-lapse nature films where seedlings broke through the earth and unwound their spindly stems and unfolded their leaves and lolled their heads in slow circles as the sun crossed the sky.

Meanwhile, Jay went on talking in a placid, soothing, conversational voice. Jay was a man of many stories, and Ryan sat there, listening as Jay held forth.

Apparently, Jay himself had once tried to fake his own death.

This was back in the days when Jay was growing up in Iowa, before he met the girl who would eventually become pregnant with Ryan.

It was the summer after ninth grade, and he had spent a lot of time planning it out. They would find his clothes and shoes in the park along the bank of the river, and he would make sure that someone had heard him screaming for help. He would hide until dark, and then he would hike south, secretly, until he was far out of town, and then he would hitch rides at truck stops until he got to Florida, and then he would stow away on a boat that was going to South America, to some city on the coast near the rain forest or the Andes, where he'd work on the tourists as a confidence man.

"It actually sounds pretty stupid, now that I think back on it," Jay said. "But at the time it seemed like a pretty good plan."

Jay chuckled, his arm still loosely draped over Ryan's shoulder. Jay leaned his face affectionately against him, and he felt the hot, dark, vegetable smell of Jay's smoky breath pass across his neck.

"I don't know," Jay said. " I guess I was feeling a lot of despair at the time—I'd been having some hard times in school. I wasn't much of a student. Not like Stacey. I was just so bored all the time, and I felt like I was disappointing everyone, and I hated my life so much—

"My parents were always putting Stacey up on a pedestal. Like she was the model for how to live, you know. I'm not trying to disrespect her achievements or anything, but you know, it was hard to take. My mom and dad would hold her up like she was this goddess. Stacey Kozelek! Stacey Kozelek got straight A's! She was so diligent! She had a *plan* for her life! And I was supposed to be, like, 'Oooooh: worship. So impressive.' "

He shrugged, reluctantly. "Not to talk down on your mom. It wasn't her fault, you know—she was a hard worker. Good for her, right? But as for me, that wasn't what I wanted. I never wanted to get to a point in my life where I knew what was going to happen next, and I felt like most people just couldn't wait until they found themselves settled down into a routine and they didn't have to think about the next day or the next year or the next decade, because it was all planned out for them.

"I can't understand how people can settle for having just one life. I remember we were in English class and we were talking about that poem by—that one guy. David Frost. 'Two roads diverged in a yellow wood—' You know this poem, right? 'Two roads diverged in a yellow wood, and sorry I could not travel both and be one traveler, long I stood and looked down one as far as I could, to where it bent in the undergrowth—'

"I loved that poem. But I remember thinking to myself: *Why?* How come you can't travel both? That seemed really unfair to me."

He paused and took a drag of his cigarette, and Ryan, who had been listening dreamily, waited. Outside, it was snowing, and he could feel his heart making a soft shushing sound in his ears.

"I didn't get very far, though," Jay said. "The cops picked me up just after midnight, walking down the highway—after curfew, and my mom and dad were there waiting for me when I got home. Pissed as hell.

"But nobody thought I was dead. They didn't even find my clothes that I'd left on the riverbank. I went back the next day, and there they were, my shoes and shirt and pants, just lying there."

As he listened to Jay talk, Ryan leaned back against the old couch and closed his eyes.

It was a relief. It was actually a relief to be dead, a lot better than committing suicide, which was what he had been considering during those fall months before Jay called him. He had known, all that semester, that he was going to fail out of college. An academic suspension, they would call it, and probably around that time his parents would find out he had wasted the money from his student loans instead of paying the college bills he owed. All that autumn, he could feel the inevitable revelations looming closer and closer, only a few weeks or months in the future, the various humiliations and the sessions in the offices of various administrators, and at last his parents' surprise and disappointment as they learned how badly he had fucked up.

Late one night in his dorm room, he had typed "painless suicide" into a search engine on the Internet and discovered an assisted-suicide society that was recommending asphyxial suicide by inhalation of helium inside a plastic bag.

He was thinking particularly about how difficult it would be to have to face his mom. She had been so happy that he had gotten into a good college. He remembered the way she had obsessed over his college application process. Starting his freshman year in high school, she had kept a chart of his grades, his GPA, how could it be improved? What activities would be most impressive? How did his achievement test scores compare, and were there improvements that could be effected by taking a summer course in How to Take Achievement Tests? What teachers—potential recommenders—

liked him? How could he make them like him more? What would he write about for his college essay? What did a successful college essay look like?

He spent a lot of time dreading the look on her face when she finally found out that he'd screwed up again—her dour watchful silence as he moved back into his old room, as they talked about community college options, or getting a job for a year or so—

It was probably easier on her, in some ways, to be presiding over his funeral.

Easier on a lot of people. He found his obituary posted online, and when he did an Internet search on his name, he saw that a lot of friends had written tributes to him on their blogs, and there was a series of touching farewell messages on his Facebook page. "Rest in peace," people said, "I will not forget you," they said, "I'm sorry that such a terrible event happened to a cool guy like you."

Which, he had to admit, was probably better than the uncomfortable, embarrassed dissipation that would have happened after he'd been sent back home to Council Bluffs in disgrace, the emails and IMs dwindling as he and his friends had less and less in common, knowing that some of them were gossiping about him or flat-out dismissing him, that guy who *flunked out*, or probably after a while he would just not be on their minds at all, their lives would roll forward and after a year or so they would have difficulty calling up his name.

Better for all involved to have this kind of closure.

Better, he thought, to start over entirely.

He had been working on putting together some new identities. Matthew Blurton was one. Kasimir Czernewski was another.

"Clones," Jay called them. Or sometimes: "Avatars." It was like when you were playing a video game, said Jay, who spent a lot of his free time wandering through the endless virtual landscapes of World of Warcraft or Call of Duty or Oblivion. "That's basically what it's like," Jay had said, and he'd fixed his eyes on the large television screen, where he was advancing on an enemy with his sword raised. "It's basically the same idea," he said. "You create your character. You maneuver them through the world. You pay attention, watch what you are doing, and you are rewarded." And then his thumbs began to work rapidly on the buttons of his game controller, as he engaged in battle.

The concept made sense, Ryan thought, though he himself was not as big of a video game person as Jay.

To Ryan, the names were more like shells—that was how he conceptualized them—hollow skins that you stepped into and that began to solidify over time. At first, the identity was as thin as gossamer: a name, a social security number, a false address. But soon there was a photo ID, a driver's license, a work history, a credit history, credit cards, purchases, and so forth. They began to take on a life of their own, developed substance. A *presence* in the world—which, in fact, was probably already more significant than the minor ripples he had created in his twenty years as Ryan Schuyler.

In fact, Ryan had already developed an attachment to Kasimir Czernewski, who had been born in Ukraine, and Ryan parted his hair down the middle and wore a pair of black glasses when he had the driver's license photo taken. Jay showed him how easy it was to establish certain other elements: a fake address—an apartment in Wauwatosa, just outside of Milwaukee; and a job, working from home as a "private investigator" with a specialty in identity theft fraud; and a taxpayer ID; and a dummy website for this fake business; and sometimes people even sent emails to Kasimir's website.

Dear Mr. Czernewski,
    I found your website and I seek help regarding the possibility of identity theft. I believe that a person or persons are using my name for the purpose of committing fraud. I have received bills for purchases that I have never made, and money is missing from several of my savings accounts, withdrawals that I never made—

As for Jay, he now had perhaps several hundred "avatars" that he had developed—practically a whole village worth of fake people, discreetly conducting various kinds of commerce from fake addresses in Fresno and Omaha; Lubbock, Texas; and Cape May, New Jersey. Basically all over the map, and layered in such a way, Jay said, interwoven so that even if one were discovered to be false, it would only lead to another counterfeit, another clone, a series of mazes that all led to dead ends.

Who would guess that these dozens of lives were emanating from a cabin in the woods north of Saginaw, Michigan?

It was snowing more heavily now, and Ryan was lucky to have arrived back at the cabin before the storm hit. The place was pretty isolated—a ways off the main highway, through a warren of county two-lane highways and up a narrow asphalt road, nothing but a tangle of trees and shadows until at last the cabin emerged, with Jay's old boxy Econoline van in the driveway.

The cabin was nondescript. A simple one-story, one-bedroom house with log siding and a screened-in porch in front with an old couch and a woodstove; it looked like one of those places weekend fishermen went to back in the 1970s, and it had the smell of damp cedar and mildewed blankets that Ryan associated with almost-forgotten Boy Scout camp buildings.

Out beyond the porch there was a clearing in the woods and the snowflakes fluttered carelessly, curiously, in little wind trails that led at last to accumulations. It hadn't been snowing in Milwaukee when he left, but it might be now. It might be snowing in Chicago, too, in Evanston where his parents would soon be arriving for his memorial service, a drowsy layer tucking itself over the tarmac of the O'Hare airport as their plane circled.

Jay had dozed off on the porch in the heat of the stove, and a cigarette was still pinched between his fingers, which Ryan reached over and gently removed, and a cylinder of cold ash broke off and fell onto the floor. "Mm," Jay said, and pressed his cheek against his own shoulder as if it were a pillow he was nuzzling.

Ryan got up and went into the living room, where a cirrus layer of smoke was still hovering over the clustered tables—dozens of computers and scanners and fax machines and other equipment—and he took a mohair blanket off of the couch and went back and draped it over Jay.

He was slightly drunk himself, slightly stoned, and he drew out another beer from the Styrofoam ice chest. He was trying not to get too anxious, but he was more and more aware that what had happened was truly permanent.

He sat down at one of the computers with his can of beer beside the keyboard and logged on to the Internet and typed his name to see if anyone else had written about his death on their blog or whatever.

But there was nothing new.

Soon, he thought, his name would call forth fewer and fewer results. The tributes would slow to a trickle in a matter of days, and before long any mention of him would be archived and pushed deeper under sedimentary layers of information and gossip and journal entries until he essentially disappeared altogether.

He was thinking about his father.

His father—his adoptive father, Owen—had been going through some mood swings during Ryan's senior year in high school, some gloomy middle-aged forty-five-year-old man thing, and while Ryan's mother obsessed about colleges and so forth, Owen had looked on wordlessly. He had gotten into the habit of the heavy sigh, and Ryan would say:

"What?"

And he would say: "Oh . . . nothing." Sigh.

One night they were standing at the kitchen sink, the two of them washing dishes, his mom in the living room watching her favorite comedy on TV, and Owen had let out another one of his melancholic exhalations.

Ryan was drying the plates and putting them away in the cabinet and he said: "What?"

Owen shook his head. "Oh . . . nothing," he said, and then he paused to contemplate the casserole dish he was scrubbing. He shrugged.

"This is stupid," Owen said. "I was just thinking: how many more times in my life will we stand here together washing dishes?"

"Mm," said Ryan—since washing dishes was not something he would miss, actually—but he was aware that Owen was in the midst of some morbid calculation.

Owen shifted. Grimaced over a stubborn bit of noodle that he was trying to scrape off. "I guess," he said, "I don't think I'll see you very much after you go off to college. That's all.

"I can see how restless you are, buddy. And there's nothing wrong with that—I'm not saying there's anything wrong with that!" Owen said. "I wish I'd been so restless, back when I was your age. The way I'm going, I probably won't even manage to see an ocean before I die. But I'll bet you'll see them all. The seven seas—and all the continents—and I just want you to know that I think that's a great thing."

"Maybe," Ryan had said then, and he felt himself stiffening into an uncomfortable formality, embarrassed by Owen's self-depreciation, his maudlin middle-aged self-pity. "I don't know," Ryan said. "I'm sure there are more dishes to be washed together," he said lightly.

But, thinking back, he couldn't help but reflect on such moments—the kitchen in the house in Council Bluffs, the dishes in the sink, specific pieces of silverware he would have been drying that he recalled now with an unexplainable fondness, specific plates—

All the *stuff* he had left behind. The black Takamine acoustic-electric dreadnought guitar Owen and Stacey had bought for his birthday; the notebook full of tabs and lyrics for songs he was trying to write; even mix CDs he'd made, these incredible mixes that now he probably couldn't re-create. It was silly—a childish, morbid nostalgia—that an ache should open up when he thought about that guitar; or when he thought about his pet turtle, Veronica, not even a real pet. What did she care about him, what did she remember?

All these objects, which were themselves like avatars—holding his old self, his old life, inside them.

Okay, he thought. He sat there staring at the computer screen, the photograph and obituary in the Council Bluffs *Daily Nonpareil.* Okay.

The life he had been leading up until now was actually over.

He would never be seen or heard from again. Not as himself, at least.

12

Lucy and George Orson were walking down the dirt road that led to the basin where the lake used to be. Nebraska was still in a drought. It hadn't rained in who knew how long, and puffs of dust rose up from beneath the edges of their foot soles.

Yet another week had passed, and still there was no sign that they would be leaving, despite George Orson's assurances. Something had gone wrong, Lucy assumed. There was some problem with the money, though he wouldn't admit it. "Don't worry," he kept telling her. "Everything is perfectly fine, just a little slower than I thought, a little more—recalcitrant." But then he let out one of his gloomy laughs, which didn't reassure her at all. It sounded so unlike him.

For the past week or so, George Orson had not been himself. This by his own admission: "I'm sorry," he would tell her, when he spaced out, when he strayed off into a distant galaxy, in a trance of private calculations.

"George," she would say, "what are you thinking about? What are you thinking about right now?"

And his eyes would regain their focus. "Nothing," he'd say. "Nothing important. I'm just feeling out of sorts. I'm not myself lately, I guess—"

Which was just a figure of speech, she knew, but it stuck with her. *Not himself,* she thought, and in fact a certain slippage was noticeable— as if, she thought, he were an actor who had begun to lose track of his character's motivation, and even his accent seemed to have changed slightly, she thought. His vowels were looser—was she imagining this?—and his enunciation wasn't as crisp and elegant.

Surely it was natural that his voice would become more casual, as he was no longer a teacher, no longer performing in front of a class. And it was natural that a person would turn out to be a little different when you really got to know them. No one was exactly what you thought they would be.

But still, she had begun to pay closer attention to such things. Perhaps, she thought, it was her own fault that she didn't know what was going on. She had been in a dreamworld for too many days now, almost two weeks' worth of watching movies, reading, fantasizing about travel. So focused on the future places that they were going to go to that she hadn't been paying attention to what was happening in the present.

For example: that morning, she had come into the bathroom and George Orson was leaning over the sink, and when he glanced up she saw that he had shaved off his beard. Actually—briefly—she didn't even recognize him, it was as if there were an unfamiliar man standing there and she'd actually let out a gasp, she'd actually flinched.

And then she saw his eyes, his green eyes, and the face had reconstituted itself: George Orson.

"Oh my God, George," she said, and put her hand to her chest. "You startled me! I hardly recognized you."

"Hmm," George Orson said, moodily. He didn't smile, or even soften his expression. He just gazed down into the sink, where his hair had made a nest in the basin.

"Sorry," he said distractedly, and ran his fingers underneath his eyes, passing his palm slowly down his bare cheeks. "Sorry to startle you."

Lucy peered at him—this new face—uncertainly. Was he—had he been crying?

"George," she said, "is there a problem?"

He shook his head. "No, no," he said. "Just—decided it was time for a change, that's all."

"You seem," she said, "upset or something."

"No, no," he said. "It's just a mood. I'll get over it."

He continued to peer at himself in the mirror, and she continued to hesitate in the doorway of the bathroom, observing warily as he lifted a pair of scissors and cut off a piece of hair, just above his ear.

"You know," she said, "it's not a great idea to cut your own hair. I know that from experience."

"Hmm," he said. "You know what I've always told you. I don't believe in regrets." He lifted his chin, examining his profile in the way a woman might examine her makeup. He made a grimace at himself. Then he smiled brightly. Then he tried to look surprised.

" 'Regrets are idle,' " he said at last. " 'Yet history is one long regret. Everything might have turned out so differently.' "

He gave his reflection a small, wistful smile.

"It's a good quote, isn't it?" he said. "Charles Dudley Warner, a very quotable old buzzard. Friend of Mark Twain. Totally forgotten, these days."

He cut off another piece of hair, this time on the other side of his head, working the scissors in a slow, ruminant line.

"George," she said, "come over here and sit down. Let me do that."

He shrugged. Whatever mood he was in had begun to dissipate— the quote, she guessed, had cheered him up, being able to name a famous person and produce some tidbit of trivia. That made him happy.

"Okay," he said, at last. "Just a trim. A little bit off the sides."

And so now, a few hours later, they were walking silently, and George Orson had taken her hand as they wended their way down the tire track grooves that were still worn into the ground, though it was clear that it had been a long time since a car had come this way.

"Listen," he said, at last, after they had gone on wordlessly for a while. "I just wanted to thank you for being patient with me. Because I know you've been frustrated, and there have been things that I haven't been able to tell you about. As much as I would like to. There are just elements that I haven't quite figured out myself yet, completely."

She waited for him to continue, but he didn't. He just kept walking, and his fingers played along the surface of her palm reassuringly.

"*Elements?*" she said. She had forgotten her sunglasses, and he had remembered his, and she squinted, exasperated, at the dark reflective circles over his eyes. "I still don't know what you're talking about," she said.

"I know," he said. He tilted his head ruefully. "I know, it sounds like bullshit, and I'm truly sorry. I know that you're nervous, and I wouldn't blame you if you're thinking about just—packing up and leaving. I mean, I'm grateful that you haven't left already. And that's why I wanted to tell you that I honestly appreciate the fact that you trust me."

"Hmm," Lucy said. But she didn't respond. She had never been the type who accepted vague assurances. If, for example, her mother had made such a speech to her in that reasonable, gently hopeful voice, Lucy would have been goaded immediately into a fury. There was plenty for her to worry about—obviously! It was ridiculous that they had been here in this place for two weeks and he still hadn't explained what he was up to. She had a right to know! Where was the money coming from? Why was it "recalcitrant"? What was he trying to "figure out," exactly? If her mother had dragged her out to the end of the world without a word of explanation, they would have been arguing constantly.

But she didn't say anything.

George Orson wasn't her mother, nor did she want him to be. She didn't want him to see her in the way her mother had seen her. Bratty. Demanding. Mouthy. A know-it-all. Immature. Impatient. These were among the qualities her mother had accused her of over the years.

And it was her mother's words she would think of when he emerged at last from the study in the late afternoon. She spent her days watching boring old movies, reading books, playing solitaire, wandering around the house and so forth, but when he finally showed his face, she tried very hard not to seem irritable.

"I'm going to make you a wonderful dinner," George Orson said. "*Ceviche de Pescado*. You're going to love it."

And Lucy looked up from watching *My Fair Lady* for the second time, as if she had been completely absorbed. As if she hadn't been in a state of grim panic for the better part of the day. She let him bend down and press his lips to her forehead.

"You're my only one, Lucy," he whispered.

She wanted to believe it.

Even now, uncertain as she was, there was the grip of his fingers along the center of her palm and the occasional brush of his shoulder against her shoulder and the sheer solidity of his body. His focused presence. A simpleminded comfort, perhaps, but nevertheless it was enough to make her calmer.

There was still the possibility that he would take care of her. *Maybe it wasn't a mistake to come here with him.* An idea shooting up a flare into the stark gray expanse of sky. *Maybe they were still going to be rich together.*

She looked down the twin tire ruts that ran through the brush, shielding her eyes from the wind and dust, making a visor out of the flat of her hand.

"Here," George Orson said, and handed her his sunglasses, and she accepted.

It's always the girls who think they are so smart, her mother had told her once. *They're always the biggest fools, in the end.*

Which was one of the reasons she hadn't left yet. The sting of those words still lingered: *Girls who think they're so smart.* And the very idea of returning to Ohio, back to the shack with Patricia. No college, no nothing. How people would laugh at her ego. Her presumption.

It wasn't as if she were being held here against her will. Hadn't George Orson always said she could leave whenever she wanted? "Listen, Lucy," he'd told her—this in the midst of one of the many evasive conversations she'd had with him about their current situation. "Listen," he said, "I understand that you're nervous, and I just want you to know, if you ever feel as if you've lost your confidence in me, even if you ever decide that this just isn't working out, you can always go home. Always. I will regretfully but respectfully buy you a plane ticket and send you back to Ohio. Or wherever you want to go."

So.

So there were alternatives, and over the past days and weeks, she had been evaluating them.

She could almost picture herself getting on a plane; she could imagine herself walking down the aisle and lowering herself at last into a narrow seat next to a smudged window. But where was she going? Back to Pompey? Off to some city? Chicago or New York or

Off to some city where she would

Blank.

It used to be that she was full of ideas about what her future would be like. She was basically a practical person, a person who planned ahead. "Ambitious," her mother had called her, and it hadn't been a compliment.

She remembered one night, not long before her parents died, when their father had been teasing Patricia about her pet rats, joking about how the rats might be keeping her from getting a boyfriend, and their mother, who had been watchfully washing dishes in the background, had stepped in abruptly.

"Larry," Lucy's mother had said sternly, "you had better be nice to Patricia." She turned, and waved a sudsy spatula emphatically. "Because I'll tell you this much: Patricia is going to be the one who will take care of you in your old age. You keep smoking like you do and you'll be wheeling around an oxygen tank by the time you're fifty-five, and it's not going to be Lucy who will be taking you to the doctor and bringing you your groceries, I can tell you that. Once Lucy is out of high school, she's going to be gone, and then you're going to be sorry you teased Patricia so much."

"Geez," Lucy's father said, and Lucy, who was studying at the kitchen table, lifted her head.

"What does this have to do with me?" she said, though her mother was essentially right. There was no way she was going to hang around Pompey, caring for a sick parent. She would pay for a nursing home, she thought. But still—it was weird of her mother to compare her to Patricia in such a way, and she leveled an offended stare in her mother's direction. "I don't know what's so wrong with wanting to go to college and maybe do something different."

At the time, she was thinking that she might go into law, corporate law was where the money was, she had heard. Or investment banking and securities: Merrill Lynch, Goldman Sachs, Lehman Brothers, one of those types of places. She could picture their shining offices, all glass and glistening wood and blue light, the wall-length windows with a Manhattan skyline hanging in the air outside. She had even downloaded information from company websites about internships and so on, though looking back it was clear they didn't give internships to high school students in Ohio.

Her mother had been surprisingly hostile about the idea. "I don't know if I could stand to have a lawyer in the family," her mother had said blithely. "Let alone a banker."

"Don't be ridiculous," Lucy said.

And her mother had sighed humorously. "Oh, Lucy," she said, and adjusted her pink hospital scrub blouse, getting ready to go off to her shift. She was just an LPN, not even a registered nurse; she hadn't even been to a real four-year college. "That stuff is all about 'What's in it for me?' It's all about money, money, money. That's not a way to live."

Lucy was silent for a moment. Then she said, softly: "Mother, you don't know what you're talking about."

Now, as she and George Orson approached the old dock, she was thinking again about leaving, thinking again about the plane lifting off toward some blank space—like a cartoon plane flying off the page into nothingness.

Or, she could stay.

She needed to think over her choices prudently. She was aware that George Orson was engaged in activity that was illegal; she was aware that there was a lot he hadn't told her—a lot of secrets. But so what? It was that secretive quality that drew her to him in the first place, why deny it? And as long as the money itself was real, as long as that part of the situation could be worked out . . .

They'd come to a building at the end of the road. A single-frame storefront, above which a sign said: GENERAL STORE & GAS in old-time letters, and below that a series of offerings were promoted: BAIT . . . ICE . . . SANDWICHES . . . COLD DRINKS . . .

It looked like it had been closed since the days of the pony express. It was the kind of place where a stagecoach would stop in an old Western.

But that was the way things were out here, she'd come to realize. The dry wind, the hard weather, the dust. It turned everything into an antique.

George Orson stood with his head cocked, listening to the faintly creaking hinge of an old sign that advertised cigarettes. His face was expressionless, and so was the face of the storefront. The windows were broken and patched with pieces of cardboard, and there was some trash, a faded candy wrapper and a Styrofoam cup and leaves and such, dancing in a ring on the oil-stained asphalt. The pumps were just standing there, dumbly.

"Hello? Is anyone home?" George Orson called.

He waited, almost expectantly, as if someone might actually respond, some ghostly voice perhaps.

"*Zdravstvuite?*" he called. His old joke. "*Konichiwa?*"

He lifted the arm of a nozzle from its cradle on the side of a gas pump and tried it experimentally. He pulled the trigger that made the gas come out of the hose, but nothing happened, of course.

"This is what the end of civilization will look like," George Orson said. "Don't you think?"

When George Orson was a child, the lake—the reservoir—was the largest body of water in the region. Twenty miles long, four miles wide, 142 feet deep at the dam.

"You have to understand," George Orson told her. "People would come from all over—Omaha, Denver, they'd drive a hundred miles to get here. When I was a kid, it was amazing. That's what's hard to imagine now: it was full of life. I remember when you could look from the top of the dam, and you couldn't even see the end of it. Just huge, especially for a poor Nebraska kid who'd never seen an ocean. Now it looks like pictures you see from Iraq. A geologist friend of mine was talking about the Euphrates drying up and showed me pictures, and it looked exactly like this."

"Hmm," she said.

This was the stuff he liked to talk about. *A geologist friend of mine*— no doubt someone he had gone to school with at Yale, once upon a time. He knew all kinds of people, all kinds of stories and trivia, which occasionally he would trot out to impress her, and which, yes, she did find pretty compelling. She herself would love to know people who would grow up to be geologists and famous authors and politicians such as George Orson's classmates had done.

Lucy had applied to three colleges: Harvard, Princeton, and Yale.

Those were the only places she was interested in, *the most famous places,* she'd thought, *the most important—*

And she could picture herself on their campuses—standing underneath the statue of John Harvard outside University Hall—hurrying through the McCosh Courtyard at Princeton with her books under her arms—or walking along Hillhouse Avenue in New Haven, "The most beautiful street in America," according to the brochures, on her way to a reception at the president's house—

She would have come across as bashful when she first arrived, and though she wouldn't have had any nice clothes, it wouldn't matter. She would've dressed simply, in dark, modest outfits that might even be thought of as mysterious. In any case, it wouldn't have been too much time before people began to recognize her, as George Orson had, for her subtle wit, her sharp sense of the absurd, her incisive comments in class. Her roommate, she thought, would probably be an heiress of some sort, and when Lucy at last shyly revealed that she was an orphan, she might be invited to spend the holidays in the Hamptons or Cape Cod or some such place—

These were not fantasies she could tell to George Orson. He was very critical of his Ivy League education—despite the fact that he mentioned it frequently. He didn't think very highly of the people he'd encountered there. "That grotesque performance of privilege," he said. "All the princes and princesses, primping while they waited to take their rightful place at the front of the line. God, how I hated them!"

He would tell her these things after they became involved, back during the spring semester of her senior year, and she would lie in his bed with her face turned away from him trying to think of how she would probably have to break things off when she went off to Massachusetts or Connecticut or New Jersey. She would have to tell him when the acceptance letters finally came, it would be painful but it would probably be for the best, ultimately.

A few days later, the first rejection had arrived in the mail. She'd discovered it when she came home from school—Patricia was at work—and she sat there at the kitchen table and she could feel her mother's collection of Precious Moments figurines staring down at her. Round-headed porcelain children with large eyes and almost no nose or mouth: reading a book together, or sitting on a giant cupcake, or holding a puppy. All of them arranged on a plastic shelving unit her mother had bought at the drugstore. She smoothed the letter out in front of her: they wished they could be writing with a different decision, they said. They wished it were possible to admit her. They hoped she would accept their best wishes.

In retrospect, she didn't know why she had been so confident. True, she had earned A's in almost all her classes—her grade point average marred by only a couple of B+ semesters in French, the gentle but unforgiving Mme Fournier, who never approved of her accent or embouchure. She had dutifully joined clubs of various sorts—the National Honor Society, Masque and Gavel, Future Business Leaders of America, Model United Nations, and so on. She had scored in the ninety-fourth percentile on the SAT.

Which, she realized now, was not nearly good enough. George Orson was right: a person would have to think in a certain calculated way from early on, from grade school, or before grade school, or, more likely, you would probably need to be groomed for it from the start. By the time you were Lucy's age . . .

The other two rejection letters had come that next week.

She knew what they were even before she looked at them. She could hear the neighbor's dog's dull, aggrieved barking outside, and at last she opened one of the letters and she could guess the contents from the first word.

"After . . ."

She laid the palm of her hand across the page and closed her eyes.

She had been doing so well. Despite her parents' deaths, despite the terrible situation of her home life, the empty refrigerator, the bills she and Patricia could barely pay, the meager income Patricia earned from the Circle K Convenience Store and the remains of their parents' insurance and the two of them eating frozen dinners and canned soups and horrible convenience store hot dogs and nachos that Patricia brought home from work—despite the fact that she didn't have a cell phone or an iPod or even a computer like most normal kids her age—

Despite everything, she had been moving forward, you could even say she'd behaved with a certain degree of dignity and grace, you might even say she was heroic, going off to school every day and doing her homework at night and writing her papers and raising her hand in class and *she had never once cried, she had never complained about what was happening to her. Didn't that count for something?*

Apparently not. Her palm was still resting across the words on the letter, and she peered down at her hand as if it were a discarded glove in a snowbank.

She had been mistaken. She could feel the realization settling over her. The life she had been traveling toward—imagining herself into—the ideas and expectations that had been so solid only a few weeks ago—this life had been erased, and the numb feeling crept up from her hand to her arm to her shoulder and the sound of the barking next door seemed to solidify in the air.

Her future was like a city she had never visited. A city on the other side of the country, and she was driving down the road, with all her possessions packed up in the backseat of the car, and the route was clearly marked on her map, and then she stopped at a rest area and saw that the place she was headed to wasn't there any longer. The town she was driving to had vanished—perhaps had never been there—and if she stopped to ask the way, the gas station attendant would look at her blankly. He wouldn't even know what she was talking about.

"I'm sorry, miss," he'd say gently. "I think you must be mistaken. I never heard of that place."

A sense of sundering.

In one life, there was a city you were on your way to. In another, it was just a place you'd invented.

This was not a period of her life she liked to remember, but she found herself thinking of it nevertheless. This was one of the things George Orson did not understand, one of the things she could never have told him about herself. She couldn't imagine describing the conversation she'd had with a "counselor" at the admissions office at Harvard—the way she'd started crying—

"You don't understand," she said, and it wasn't just that a little sob or whimper had escaped her—it was as if her whole body were draining and becoming hollow, a thick needles-and-pins sensation ran down through her scalp and over her face, and her heart and lungs tightened. "I don't have anything," she said. "I'm an orphan," she said, and the sensation had gone from her lips and for some reason she thought maybe she could possibly go blind. Her fingers were shaking. "My mother and father are dead," she said, and a ragged, heavy space seemed to open up beneath her throat.

This was what real grief felt like—she had never truly felt it before. All the times she had been sad, all the times she had wept in her life, all the glooms and melancholies were merely moods, mere passing whims. Grief was a different thing altogether.

She let the phone slide down and she put her hand to her mouth as an awful and soundless breath came out of it.

And a few weeks later, when George Orson suggested that she leave town with him, it felt like the only reasonable thing to do.

They'd reached the edge of the boat ramp, a cement slope that led
down into the basin of the former lake, and there was a battered
sign that said:

NO SWIMMING OR WADING
WITHIN 20 FEET OF RAMPS OR DOCKS

"I've been meaning to show you this," George Orson said, ges-
turing out toward some point in the sandy expanse of flatland and
scrubby weeds, where the water had once been.

"I don't see anything," Lucy said.

She'd been inside her own head for a while by that time, growing bleaker as their path descended, but of course George Orson
couldn't read her thoughts. He didn't know that she was remembering the great humiliation of her life; he didn't know that she was
thinking about leaving; he couldn't hear her wondering whether
there was any money in the house.

Though naturally he could read her mood; she could see how
he was trying to entertain her. Now it was his turn to try to cheer *her*
up. "Just wait. You'll like this," he said, clasping her hand, his voice
brightening as he guided her along.

Her own private history teacher.

"Down this way is where the town was," he said, and he gestured
like a lecturer as they walked. "Lemoyne," he said. "That was what it
was called. It was a small village, and when they decided to make the
reservoir back in the 1930s, the state bought up all the land and the
houses and relocated the people, and then they flooded it. It's not
a unique phenomenon, actually. There are, I would guess, hun-
dreds of them all across the United States. 'Drowned towns'—
I think that's the term. As the technology for creating these irriga-
tion and hydroelectric reservoirs advanced, the people just had to
move aside—"

And he paused, checking to see if he still had her attention.

"Such is progress," he said.

She saw it now. The town. Or rather, what was left of it, which was not particularly townlike after all. The dust was blowing hard in the basin, and the structures ahead were blurred, as if in fog.

"Wow," she said. "This is weird."

"Nebraska's own Atlantis," George Orson said, and glanced at her, gauging her reaction. She could see him planning out what he was going to say, then reconsidering.

"There's a lot of energy here," George Orson said, and he gave her one of his intense, secretive smiles. He was teasing, but he was also serious in a way she didn't quite understand.

"Energy," she said.

His smile broadened—as if she knew exactly what he was getting at. "Energy of the supernatural variety. So they say. They list it in all of those hokey books—*America's Most Haunted, Mysterious Places of the Great Plains,* you know what I mean. Not to say that I discount it wholesale. But I guess if there is energy, it's probably mostly negative, I'd imagine. Not too far from here is where the Battle of Ash Hollow happened. This was back in 1855, and General William Harney led six hundred soldiers onto a Sioux encampment and massacred eighty-six people, many of them women and children. It was part of President Pierce's plan, you see, the westward expansion, the Oregon Trail, the growth of the U.S. Army—"

Lucy frowned. She had been hoping for more about their current situation, but it appeared that this was just another one of his distractions. More chitchat about the things that he found fascinating—cheesy-sounding new age philosophy mixed up with conspiratorial antigovernment historical analysis—though at one time she'd liked it when he would hold forth on such stuff, not least because then she could play the part of the skeptic.

"Oh, right," she said now, and let herself touch once again on their bantering voice, the way they used to talk to each other, the earnest teacher and the wryly challenging student.

"I suppose there are probably secret alien UFO landing bases right around here, too," she said.

"Ha, ha," he said.

And then he pointed, and she felt the back of her neck prickle.

Up ahead, there were perhaps a dozen buildings, rising up among the silt and sand and big tumbleweed-shaped bushes and scrub grass, though "buildings" wasn't exactly the right term.

Remains, she thought. Pieces of structures in various states of collapse and ruin—foundations and scattered slabs of cement—a fat hexagonal block, an oblong column, a triangular corner piece—all with tails of sand pulling behind them. There was a single rocky wall with the rectangle of a door in it. The detritus of an old outhouse or shed had heaved itself over into a pile of rotting boards, covered in silt and algae, and beyond it a crooked, rusted street sign was still posted. At the end of what she guessed had once been the street, there was a larger four-walled frame, some steps leading up the front of the stone block façade.

"Holy shit, George," she said.

Which had always been another part of their relationship. She was the cynic and he was the believer, but she could be persuaded. She could be brought to a state of wonder, if only he was convincing enough.

And he had succeeded this time.

"That was the church," George Orson said. They stood there together, side by side, and she thought that actually he was right about "negative energy," or whatever.

"Doesn't this seem like a good place to perform a ritual?" George Orson said.

And she was aware again of that feeling, that end-of-the-world stillness. She thought of what George Orson had told her back when they were driving through Indiana or Iowa and she was still vaguely talking about going to college: she'd apply again in a year or so, she'd said.

"I wouldn't bother if I were you," George Orson had said, and he'd looked over at her, his lopsided smile pulling up. "By the time you're forty, it's not going to matter whether you graduated from college or not. I doubt if Yale University will even exist."

And Lucy had given him a stern look. "Oh, right," she said. "And apes will rule the earth."

"Honestly," George Orson said. "I'm not so sure there will even be a United States by that point. At least not as we know it."

"George," she said, "I have no idea what you're talking about."

But now, standing in the dried-out basin of the lake, on the steps of the old church where the body of a carp had mummified among a clump of cobwebbed moss—now she could easily imagine the United States was already gone; the cities were burnt and the highways glutted with rusting cars that had never made it out of town.

"It's funny," George Orson was saying. "My mother used to tell us you could see the steeple underneath the water when it was clear—which was a myth, naturally, but my brother and I used to come out here on the pontoon and dive down, looking for it. We're probably about—what would you say?—pretty close to the middle of the lake, and you have to imagine that it was fairly deep at the time. Twelve or thirteen fathoms?"

He was in his own dreamy state, and she watched his finger as he lifted it and pointed upward. "Think about it!" he said. "About seventy or eighty feet above us, there would be the boat, and you could see the two of us dive into the water. You'd be like a shark down here watching the legs splashing and you'd see the surface of the water up there—"

Yes. She could see it. She could imagine being at the bottom of the lake—the membrane of the water hovering above them like the surface of a sky, and the rippled shadow of the pontoon boat, and the figures of the boys in the diffuse blue-green light, their silhouettes like birds skimming the air.

She shuddered, and the fantasy of water and childhood nostalgia drained away.

The pale dust was blowing in horizontal streams close to the ground, snaking in thin, rippling pathways that built tombolos off the scrub plants. All the color around her was washed out by the dust and glare, like a photograph with the brightness and contrast turned up too high.

There was nothing like that in her own childhood, no idyllic vacations at a beach, no pontoon boats or mysterious underwater towns. She could remember summer days at the Pompey swimming pool, or running through the sprinkler in the yard with Patricia, Patricia a plump little girl in a one-piece bathing suit, her mouth open to catch the spray of water.

Poor Patricia, she thought.

Poor Patricia, washing the dishes and doing the laundry and looking sorrowfully at Lucy as she sat there on the couch watching TV. As if she were too good to clean up after herself. Perhaps, Lucy thought, it was better for both of them that she was gone. Maybe Patricia was happier.

"So," Lucy said. "Where is your brother now? Do you ever call him, or talk to him or anything?"

George Orson blinked. He was coming back from some memory himself, she guessed, because at first he was taken aback. As if the question puzzled him. Then he straightened.

"He's—actually he's not around anymore," George Orson said at last. His forehead creased. "He drowned. Somewhere—I guess about five miles north of here. He was eighteen. It was the year he graduated from high school, and I was in college, I was still in New Haven, and apparently—" He paused, as if he were straightening a painting in a room in his mind.

"Apparently, he went out for a swim at night, and—that was it. What happened, it's impossible to know, because he was alone, but they never did figure out *why*. He was an excellent swimmer."

"You're not joking," she said.

"Of course not," he said, and gave her one of his gently re-proachful looks. "Why would I joke about something like that?"

"Jesus, George," she said, and they fell mute, both of them look-ing up to the narrow slate-colored cirrus clouds that were laid across the sky. The former surface of the water, twelve fathoms above them.

She wasn't sure what to think. How long had they been to-gether? Almost five months? All those hours and hours of conver-sations, all the talk of various kinds of history and movies and his years at Yale and his geologist friend and his magician friend and the crazy computer guys from Atlanta, all this flotsam and jetsam, and yet she couldn't have put together even a basic biography of his life.

"George," she said, "don't you think it's weird that you never told me that you had a brother who died?"

She was trying to maintain their usual bantering tone, but her voice hitched, and she had the awful feeling that she might be over-come by another crying fit such as she had on that day she called the admissions counselor on the phone. She paused; tightened her mouth. "I told you about *my* parents," she said.

"Yes, you did," George Orson said. "And you know, I've always appreciated that you've been so forthright." He shrugged mildly; he didn't want to argue, he didn't want her to be upset. His expres-sion flickered, uncertainly, and she wondered if he had been caught in a truth—the same way some people were caught in a lie.

"Honestly?" he said. "I didn't think you needed to hear any more tragic death stories. With your own loss still weighing so heavily on you? You needed to get away from all that, Lucy. You told me about your parents—you did. But you didn't really want to talk about it."

"Hmm," she said—because perhaps he was right; maybe he did understand her, after all. Was it possible that she was as lost as he seemed to think she was?

"Besides which," he said, "my brother died a long time ago. I don't find myself thinking about it very often. Most of the time, only when I'm out here."

"I see," she said, and they sat down together on the crumbling steps of the old church. "I see," she said again, and here was that pitch in her voice again, that tremor. She thought of that one time when her father took her and Patricia fishing on Lake Erie, the boat with the sonar scanner that would help them find the big fish. She could imagine George Orson sounding his memory, locating the shadow of his brother, sliding through the dark water.

"But—don't you miss him?" she said.

"I don't know," George Orson said at last. "Of course I miss him, in a certain way. I was very upset when he died, naturally; it was a terrible tragedy. But—"

"But what?" Lucy said.

"But fourteen years is a long while," George Orson said. "I'm thirty-two years old, Lucy. You might not realize that yet, but you pass through a lot of different stages in that amount of time. I've been a lot of different people since then."

"A lot of different people," she said.

"Dozens."

"Oh, really?" she said. And she was aware of that wavering shadow passing over her once again, all the different people she herself had wanted to become, all the sadness and anxiety that she had been trying not to think about now shifting above her like an iceberg. Were they merely bantering again? Or were they in the midst of a serious conversation?

"So—" she said. "So—who are you right now?"

"I'm not sure exactly," George Orson said, and he looked at her for a long time, those green eyes moving in minnow darts, scoping her face. "But I think that's okay."

She let him run his palm over the back of her hand. Across her knuckles, her fingers, her nails, her fingertips. He touched her leg, the way he always did when he was particularly focused on her.

He did love her, she thought. For whatever reason, it felt like he was probably the only person left who truly knew her. The real her.

"Listen," George Orson said. "What if I told you that you could leave your old self behind? Right now. What if I told you we could bury George Orson and Lucy Lattimore, right here. Right in this little dead town."

He wasn't dangerous, she thought. He wouldn't hurt her. And yet his face, his eyes, had such an odd, unnerving intensity. She wouldn't have been surprised if he was going to tell her that he had done something terrible. Murdered someone, maybe.

Would she still love him, would she still stay with him, if he had committed some awful crime?

"George," she said, and she could hear how hoarse and uncertain her voice sounded, down in this valley. "Are you trying to scare me?"

"Not at all," George Orson said, and he took her palms in his and held them firmly and drew his face close to hers, so that she could see how bright and avid and earnest his eyes were. "No, honey, I swear to God, I would never try to scare you. Never."

And then he smiled at her, hopefully.

"It's just that—oh, sweetheart, I don't think I can be George Orson for much longer. And if we're going to stay together, you can't be Lucy Lattimore much longer, either."

Across the weedy lake bed, the clouds were stacked above the opposite shore, dirty white fading upward into dark gray. A vapor of dust stirred up across the valley where there were once fathoms of water.

13

Miles was sitting in a bar in Inuvik when his phone rang.

He was hovering over his fourth beer, and at first he wasn't sure where the sound was coming from—just a tiny computerized twitter of birdsong that seemed to be emanating from an undisclosed location in the air around him. He glanced at the bartender, and then over his shoulder, and then at the floor below his bar stool, and then at last he discovered the chirping was actually the phone in his jacket pocket.

This was the phone he had purchased at the local wireless place—Ice Wireless, it was called—since he had realized his own phone couldn't get reception. One of the many things he hadn't taken into account when he left Cleveland. One of the many expenditures that had been added to his credit card over the years, in search of Hayden.

But here: this time it turned out to be worth it. The phone was actually ringing.

"Hello?" he said, and there was a blank sound. "Hello? Hello?" he said. He wasn't used to this phone yet, wasn't sure if he was operating it correctly.

Then there was a woman's voice. "I'm calling about the poster?" she said, and at first he was so flustered to encounter a voice at the other end of the phone that synapses in his brain stumbled over one another.

"The poster . . . ?" he said.

"Yes," the woman said. "There was a flyer—a missing person—and this was the number that it said to call. I think I have information about the person on the poster." She had an American accent, the first one he'd heard in a while, and he straightened, patting his pockets for a pen.

"I believe I know the person you're looking for," she said.

He was a terrible detective.

That was one of the things he had been thinking about on the drive to Inuvik. He had spent the entire decade of his twenties looking for Hayden—sleepwalking through various odd jobs and attempts at higher education—and all the while thinking that his "real" vocation was elsewhere. His real vocation was "detective," his real vocation was looking for Hayden, he'd thought, his every attempt at normalcy punctuated—punctured—by periods of intense Hayden-obsession: gathering and sifting through data, spending his money and charging up credit cards so that he could go on these long, fruitless trips.

Though in fact, the truth was, in all these years, he'd done little but accumulate endless notebooks full of unanswered questions:

Is Hayden schizophrenic? Does he have a mental illness, or is that an act?

Unknown.

Does Hayden really believe in his "past lives," and if so, how is that related to his study of "ley lines," "geodesy," and "spirit cities"? Or is this, too, a scam?

Unknown.

Was Hayden responsible for the house fire that killed our mother and Mr. Spady?

Unknown.

Why was Hayden in Los Angeles, and what was the nature of his "residual income stream consultant" business?

Unknown.

What was the nature of his graduate work in mathematics at the University of Missouri, Rolla? How did he get accepted into graduate school when he hadn't even completed an undergraduate degree?

Unknown.

What happened to the young woman he was dating in Missouri?

Unknown.

What, if any, is Hayden's relationship with H&R Block, Morgan Stanley, Lehman Brothers, Merrill Lynch, Citigroup, etc.?

Unknown.

Why did Hayden warn about Mrs. Matalov/Matalov Novelties?

Unknown.

Why is Hayden in Inuvik? Is Hayden in Inuvik?

Unknown.

He sat there at the bar, staring at his spiral reporter's notebook, into which he had printed these and other questions in neat block letters, *his* handwriting, which, ever since childhood, had been a pale imitation of Hayden's more elegant script.

He held the phone to his ear.

"Yes," he said. "You have information about the—the person—the poster?" He was aware that he sounded somewhat incredulous, and he wavered. The woman said nothing.

"We're—as the poster says, we're, ah—prepared to offer a reward," Miles said.

Reward. He supposed he could get another cash advance on his credit card.

He was still addled. Eighty-four hours, with a few sessions of sleeping in the car alongside the road—curled up in the backseat with his knuckles pressed against his mouth, a thin blanket tucked at his neck. Once, he'd awakened and he'd had the notion that he was seeing the aurora borealis in the sky, a wispy, winding smokelike shape, a glowing fluorescent-green, though this was also the color he imagined a UFO would give off as it hovered over you.

By the time he had finally arrived in Inuvik, he was in an out-of-body state. He'd taken a room in a downtown motel—the Eskimo Inn—thinking he would pass out the minute he lay down on the bed.

It was late, but the sun was still shining. The midnight sun, he thought—a dim, dull, yellowy light, as if the world were a basement room lit by a bare forty-watt bulb—and he drew the blackout curtains and sat down on the bed.

His ears were ringing, and his skin felt as if it were lightly shimmering. The buzz of his car's wheels on asphalt had worked its way inside his body, forward movement, forward movement, forward movement, and he wished that he'd had the presence of mind to buy some beer before he checked in—

Instead of sitting there, blinking stupidly, with the old atlas in his lap. A terrible detective, he thought. *Dominion of Canada,* the atlas said, the building block rectangles of Alberta, Saskatchewan, Mani-